Moondust Media

Donnalnk Publications, L.L.C.

A FLOWER GROWS

Printed in United States of America

Moondust Media

Credit: *Museum of the Banjica Concentration Camp* - formed in the complex of the old barracks, between I94I and I944, the Nazi occupier committed a large number of crimes - approximately 4.200 detainees were executed, most of them Serbs, I.000 Jews and Romas. Shooting was carried out systematically, in the camp and in Jajinci. In I969, in front of the building of the camp, a memorial was built, with the verses of Svetozar Trebjesanin, and on that occasion a memorial room was also opened.

A FLOWER GROWS

JOHN R. LORETTO

CAROLYN KAY DOSWELL

Moondust Media | DonnaInk Publications

An imprint of DonnaInk Publications, L.L.C.
17611 Aquasco Road, Brandywine, MD 20613

Library of Congress Cataloging-in-Publication:

Name(s): Doswell, Carolyn Kay and Loretto, John.

Title: "Flower Grows, A" / Ms. Carolyn Kay Doswell and Mr. John Loretto

284 p. cm.

Book cover and interior design: Ms. Donna L. Quesinberry, dpInk Ltd. Liability. Identifiers on KDP: ISBN – 13 – 978-1-947704-07-7 (alk. paper); ISBN – 13 – 978-1-947704-08-4 (digital); and ISBN – 13 – 978-1-947704-07-7 (hardback).

Subjects: BISAC: FIC014050 FICTION / Historical / World War II; FIC027050 FICTION / Romance / Historical / General; FIC027570 FICTION / Romance / Enemies to Lovers; FIC027200 FICTION / Romance / Historical / 20th Century; FIC027610 FICTION / Romance / Love Triangle; FIC040000 FICTION / Alternative History; FIC046000 FICTION / Jewish; FIC027220 FICTION / Romance / Military; FIC027110 FICTION / Romance / Suspense; FIC032000 FICTION / War & Military.

Printed in the United States of America
Edition: 12 11 10 9 8 7 6 5 4 3 2 | 2019. All Rights Reserved.

For more information, contact:

DonnaInk Publications, L.L.C.
17611 Aquasco Road, Brandywine, MD 20613
(301) 888-2414 | donnaink@gmail.com
www.donnaink.net | www.donnalquesinberry.com } www.donnaink.shop

DEDICATION

IN MEMORY OF MY GRANDFATHER, Roberto Gonzalez.

— John Loretto

TABLE OF CONTENTS

FOREWORD

HISTORIANS OF THE Holocaust have established sharp categories: perpetrator, victim, and bystander. Philosophers have introduced nuance, perhaps even confusion, by describing the "grey zone," that zone in between black and white, fully good and fully bad. One of the attractions to the Holocaust is that the perpetrators appear as evil incarnate, radical evil—mass murderers, demonic, sadistic—and the victims appear innocent, victimized not because of what they did, but by the accident of their birth as Jews. A Flower Grows is a novel about the grey zone, the world of the in between.

A word about the story: a young Serbian Jewish couple and their entire family and guest party are taken from the synagogue celebration on their wedding day, even before the consummation of their marriage, and shipped off to a slave labor camp in the former Yugoslavia. One of the bride's captors, a German officer from the educated class, spots the beautiful woman and has her brought into his home where he beds her and, over time, falls in love with her. The bride is mindful of her situation, compromised as it is, and uses it to protect as best as possible her family, who turn a blind eye to the relationship and/or tacitly consent to it to save themselves and her from almost certain death.

Whether a victim of the Stockholm syndrome – of identifying with her captors –, overtaken by sexual lust—he is handsome, she is a beautiful virgin—or merely engaged in a mutually exploitative relationship with a man who in these circumstances is all powerful, the living arrangement is sustained over time. Pregnancy follows, so too a child, and now the officer is in love and protective of his lover and their offspring.

Under ordinary circumstances one might cry out in judgment: "rape," "adultery," "exploitation," "have you—all of you, the officer, the bride, her family—no shame?" And yet the Holocaust was anything but ordinary and the grey zone is truly grey. The officer is a perpetrator, but not only a perpetrator. He is also a rescuer who risks his freedom, his career, and perhaps even his life for the woman he lusts for and ultimately loves and protects her family. Germans turned a blind eye toward the rape of Jewish women, but sustained affairs were not to be countenanced. Though present in the camp, the officer— or so he claims— tries to avoid participating in the atrocities that are the daily lot of all who enter its gates. He proclaims himself an anti-Nazi and yet he enables others to kill. He is more than merely complicit. His role is indispensable and thus far from peripheral to a killing machine. His humanity is further complicated by his tenderness toward his lover, son, and his parents.

The bride is an innocent victim, at least at the beginning, taken from the bridal canopy to a concentration camp. Ambitious, tempestuous, competitive, but still sexually innocent, she struggles as all struggled to go from a home of middle-class privilege to a concentration camp. The attraction between the officer and the bride is mutual.

Did she invite it?

What is the moment of consent?

What is her allegiance to her groom?

What are her feelings of betrayal?

The writers don't judge, they explore; they raise questions even without resolving them. The post-war ending, which I will not describe for fear of giving away the ending, is ambiguous. Part of the power of this work is that the questions are deepened, the answers harder to find. Such is the truth of what they describe. In fact, very few survivors could be so candid of their past. It would be too painful. Too dangerous.

The authors' depiction of the circumstances is accurate and their insights quite on the mark. And their readers are left to contemplate not merely a story but the heart of the grey zone to sort out the good and the bad, not an easy task indeed.

Dr. Michael Berenbaum

American scholar, professor, rabbi, writer, filmmaker & former:
Deputy Director - President's Holocaust Commission
Project Director - United States Holocaust Memorial Museum
Director of USHMM's Holocaust Research Institute
CEO / President - Survivors Shoah Visual History Foundation
Director - Sigi Ziering Institute

PREFACE

THE **PRESENT-DAY** Balkans, or Balkan Peninsula, in South Eastern Europe with Greece at its tip, is the site of the former Yugoslavia. This expanded into Serbia in 2003, after a lingering civil war, which began to smolder following the death of its unifying force President Tito who died in 1980.

Winston Churchill once said, 'The Balkans produce more history than they can possibly consume.' Spoken with a deeper meaning, that turmoil churns on a never-ending wheel.

The Balkans have been the gateway to and from the Middle East for thousands of years. In the fourteenth century, the Ottoman Turks officially moved into the Balkans bringing with them the Islamic religion, language and culture. Thusly well entrenched themselves until the Christian Austro-Hungarian Empire from the north also began to occupy part of the Balkans igniting turf and religious wars that continue to flame in modern times.

Yugoslavia, originally created in 1918 after WWI out of several different Balkan states, faced many deep divisions with the three major religions facing off. These included fully settled generational Jews. With these ethnic, religious and language divides, chaos became the norm in the Balkans. The Serbian Christians were the most resented because of their large population numbers and political domination.

ACKNOWLEDGEMENTS

CONTENTS OF THIS novel benefit from research completed by Carolyn Kay Doswell and John Loretto. Special thanks are extended to the liturgy of researchists who have documented the Holocaust since the travesty of its gruesome occurrence.

Holocaust victims' suffering, sustained by execrable German captors, is especially acknowledged. "A Flower Grows," would not exist if it weren't for this chapter of history. Both authors would have preferred not to have been enabled to pen this title if it weren't for history.

Recognition and acknowledgement are extended by both authors to the human spirit, where even in the direst circumstan-ces, when hope would seemingly be unequivocally lost forever – the characters in, "A Flower Grows" demonstrate the resilience of growth and life itself. Even the antagonist, as a German Officer, strives to make the most of his lot in life and in loving the protagonist demonstrates a counter-reality that sustains him while he answers his call of duty. Of course, this also goes against the grain of his own humanity and that confusion is explored in this novel. The same can be said for the woman he loves, who sustains her family through self-sacrifice, which goes against all her training in their systems of belief and life practice.

The authors acknowledge humanity's innate ability to achieve the best outcome in every situation – even the most deplorable from the annals of history itself.

In addition to Holocaust victims, both John Loretto and Carolyn Kay Doswell want to acknowledge **Moon**dust **Media**, an Imprint of Donna**Ink Publications, L.L.C.** for their due diligence and professsionalism.

John and Carolyn also want to thank Judith Moose for her assistance with the first edition of, "A Flower Grows" and also Eric Canton and Judith Moose for their help in generating interest in, "A Flower Grows" screenplay that is showing positive results toward film production.

Last, but certainly not least, special thanks go to Dr. Michael Berenbaum for reading, reviewing and creating the foreword to our novel. Dr. Berenbaum's extensive foreword and review represents to readers the authenticity and much needed story about the "Grey Zone" as well as Banjica Concentration Camp that has never been disclosed previously in a work such as this.

Of course, both Carolyn and John extend our sincere thank you to loyal readers who support our work and take their time to read, "A Flower Grows."

EPIGRAPH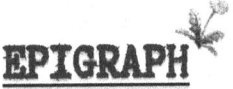

THE **THINGS I** saw beggar description... the visual evidence and the verbal testimony of starvation, cruelty, and bestiality were so overpowering as to leave me a bit sick. In one room, where there were piled up twenty or thirty naked men, killed by starvation, George Patton would not even enter. He said he would get sick if he did so. I made the visit deliberately, in order to be in a position to give first-hand evidence of these things if ever, in the future, there develops a tendency to charge these allegations merely to "propaganda."

Dwight D. Eisenhower
Former President of the United States of America

A FLOWER GROWS

CHAPTER ONE

GERMANY – 1935
A young fair skinned German girl with her head shaved stumbles through the crowded city streets. Three German SS officers accompany her, pushing and pulling her back to her feet each time she sinks to the ground in exhaustion. A crowd of nearly two hundred German working-class people wearing warm but tattered clothes yell and harass her as she stumbles by in a modern-day witch hunt.

'Die Hure, Luder, Bitch!' the angry crowd screams waving their fists at her.

The sobbing German girl drags herself along in a tattered, ripped peasant dress that clings to her hunched over body in the cold air. Glimpses of her breasts peek through the torn lace bodice exciting a male frenzy of sexually mixed sadistic aggression. A placard is attached to her chest declaring: I GIVE MYSELF TO A JEW.

Several adolescent boys in the crowd pick up small stones and hurl them at the hapless girl. One rock hits her forehead dead center, causing her to fall to the ground.

One of the menacing German SS officers forces her to her feet, trying to push her along as the heckling, barbaric parade continues. The girl is limp with a bleeding head wound. He shakes her, but she is either passed out or dead.

Somewhere in the near future World War II looms. Nailed to buildings and walkways are posters of RASSENSCHANDE (racial defilement or shame) naming the illegal pollution of white Aryan blood with Jewish blood in severe hatred. This would later include

Gypsies, Negroes and their bastard offspring. The posters are a clear and direct warning for German women to refrain from any sexual relations with Jewish men. However, there are no such threatening posters warning German men to refrain from similar relations with Jewish women. The Nuremberg Laws introduced by Hitler in 1935 state this edict clearly. Heinrich Himmler would later prove that boys will be boys. The toleration of the white German male and his frenzied libido is overwhelmingly accepted. Their lust for sex with indiscriminate women and girls will go on discretely and secretly no matter what, to hell with the law.

It's 1938 and Shayna Weinberg is only fourteen years old. She runs like the spring wind, always taking first place in any track meet at her small town's public middle school in Yugoslavia, Europe. Her best event is the fifty-yard dash and she inevitably leaves the other girls standing in her dust, glaring at her in speechless wonder. Attitude in place, Shayna feels confident. *What am I supposed to do, give up the race to the laziest? If the other girls can't run then they should get some discipline. They should train everyday like me and take better care of themselves.* With a nod of confirmation, the gym coach once again hands Shayna another first-place blue ribbon.

Shayna's best friend in school is Rachel Cohen who is equal to Shayna in beauty and brains, but not in the fierce determination of Shayna's racing resolve. Rachel likes running too, but to her it's more of a social encounter to be seen and grab attention for the notoriety of a popular school athlete to enjoy.

Both girls are in the same grade and often share lunches together in the cafeteria. Shayna most often packs her food at home, rejecting the school's high fat and sugar laden low-priced meals. "I try not to eat the heavy starchy foods served here because it's fattening. A fat girl can't walk not to mention run." Shayna opens her brown lunch bag and brings out cooked beans on rye bread and a sack of carrots and celery. Yesterday it was peanut butter on wheat bread and an apple. She washes it all down with plain water or fruit juice, even rejecting the school's heavy mucous drinks like milk. "A runner's body is like a fine-tuned engine. You can't throw down low grade oil or you will clog the engine with garbage." Shayna wheezes out with a little chuckle at her own analogy. Rachel nods, smiling in silent agreement. "I'll never understand why those girls who compete with me keep eating and eating until their legs scrape together like dough when they walk," Shayna states with a shrug. Rachel laughs at her as she skims over her cafeteria food with a fork. "Just look at that sausage," Shayna points at Rachel's plate. "Now, why would I want that meaty fat on my hips for twenty years?" Shayna's face turns down in revulsion. "I'd have to haul that bloated sausage around the track with me... clump de clump." Rachel giggles and pushes her lunch plate away. Shayna finally relaxes and takes a bite of her sandwich. "This is what I do," Shayna blinks her eyes at Rachel in firm commitment. "I stay healthy and fit so I can be electricity and fly down the wires with my hair standing straight up."

The previous year Shayna was offered the much sought-after position of school cheerleader. She refused it telling the squad coach that her energy and ambition was not meant to be given away to the boys. It was for her endeavors. If that was deemed unpatriotic to the school and personally selfish, they needed to start respecting their own gender more.

The coach had absolutely nothing to say to Shayna. She walked away perplexed with brow wrinkled, amazed that such a young girl could be so insightful into her surroundings, and strong enough to follow her own direction with such resolve. Shayna knowingly lived in her own brand of self-awareness but condemned herself to middle school social isolation where twisted, immature logic ostracizes anyone. Strong willed girls who are different in any way from the common norm and expected patterns of behavior for girls are especially so.

Shayna gets up an hour early every school day so she can run on the school track with her high-flying bird friends. They chirp their ritual of morning odes to the magnificence of the rising sun bringing a new day. On weekends, she usually runs through her neighborhood or sometimes in the nearby park. She buzzes by the morning walkers like a swift little plane that flies with a faraway hum in the sky for just a few minutes and then it's gone. She gives the walkers only a fleeting glimpse into the mystery of such extraordinary exuberance.

This morning about ten eager, screaming boys are on the school's field practicing soccer. Two or three are hoarding the ball while charging and crashing into each other. Only two are shooting hoops on the basketball court and surprisingly they are girls who were previously banned from participation in this low impact sport. They are now being slowly integrated into their own teams where they are learning sport's competition and team bonding. Shayna notices and appreciates this important gender shift toward fairness and sports equality for girls but still prefers to run alone. However, occasionally the other girls will show up hoping that some of Shayna's positive enthusiasm and winning streak would somehow rub off.

Rachel waits at the track entrance and Shayna greets her with friendly zeal despite the fact all Rachel really wants to do is talk about boys. Shayna listens for several minutes, allowing Rachel her talk and venting time for her latest boy troubles. Shayna, however, is on a mission to run and train; nothing much ever stops her.

"Rachel, I think that you should just forget about that egotistical Ron Kaiser. He's big in freshman soccer but little in respect. All he ever really talks about is how important he is to our school. Even if you marry him someday and he goes on to become a pro, he probably will just treat you the same way that he does now."

"I don't think so, Shayna." Rachel snaps back, rejecting any constructive criticism. She is obviously ready to make excuses for him.

"Fine Rachel, whatever you say, but I have to train today and that Kaiser kid you date is just wasting both our time. Can't you just forget about him and run for a while?"

"But he's in my first period history class." Rachel whines out as if she's helpless.

"Okay Rachel, if that's all you want out of life." Shayna abruptly turns around and starts running at a slow pace, gradually picking up speed. She glances back several times to see if Rachel is going to run, but Rachel ignores her. Instead she stumbles off into the bleachers like a forgotten heroine in last year's school play. She drops onto a seat, hanging her head as if waiting for the invisible strings of her boyfriend, puppet master Ron Kaiser, to lift it.

Later that same day in fourth period language arts class, Shayna watches as Rachel falls into a love trance. She ignores the teacher's lesson presentation and concentrates only on Ron Kaiser who sits across the classroom from her. He is talking to the girl beside him and Rachel is on the verge of exploding into a jealous rage. Shayna shakes her head in amazement wondering how her best friend's hormones had gotten so out of whack.

Why does she let this silly young boy control and take advantage of her?

CHAPTER TWO

AS THE GERMAN Army expands its war machine across Europe, April 1941, brings an easy victory. It also brings a losing battle to the Royal Yugoslav Army. It gives up its army headquarters and barracks to the German Fascist expansion and partially puts to rest the power of the Yugoslavian Monarchy, at that time ruled by King Peter II. The German Army demonstrates its total occupation with a formal march through the capital city of Belgrade, Yugoslavia. Hundreds of German troops slam polished boots against the roadway pavement. They arrogantly display pressed, decorative Nazi swastikas on impeccably starched uniforms with matching hats as they march through the shaking streets of Belgrade with a raging fervor never before witnessed.

Hundreds of Yugoslavian citizens gather along the sidewalks and byways, welcoming the invading Germans with loud robust cheers and Nazi salutes. It is more than a miscarriage of justice. It is a sad, regressive day for the human race. Only days before the invading Germans had killed nearly seventeen thousand civilians in Belgrade alone within the first twenty–four hours of their attack. It then took the Germans only eleven additional days to force a Yugoslavian surrender.

Both women and men hold up their young children as the German troops enter claiming Yugoslavia in a certain, forceful dominance of occupation. The smiling civilians show no signs of regret or sorrow that their country is defeated, and thousands murdered. They open their arms and hearts as if their saviors had finally arrived. Only a handful of onlookers hang their heads in fear mixed with loathing. They fall back behind the cheering crowds, slowly fading into the cracks and crannies. They hide like roaches awaiting an uncertain and terrifying future.

Mountains have always provided a sense of secret. Shamans usually live in houses on the edge of the woods so that they can have access to both the physical and spiritual worlds.

The true saviors of war are the Yugoslav partisans. They are a local group of multiethnic rebel fighters who oppose the Germans and their Serbian collaborators. After German occupation, the Yugoslavian Serbian bureaucracy quickly becomes puppets to the Nazi war machine. These Serbian military collaborators carry out all orders including destruction of any other Serb or local Slavic peasant who refuses to cooperate, obey or subject themselves or their families to the present German military orders. If they are Communists, they are shot immediately.

It is June of 1941 just two months after German occupation. Hidden somewhere in the mountains of Yugoslavia, the rebel partisans begin banding together to plan a strategy for military coups. The partisans presently are about one hundred multiethnic soldiers. They are wearing a mixture of light brown military uniforms with street clothes, heavy boots and carry various items of military gear. They remain mostly a semi-trained volunteer military recruitment consisting of Yugoslavians, Jews, civilian Serbians, Croats, other local ethnic Slavs and a few Muslims. While different, they are all driven by a concerted hatred of Hitler and his Serbian goons. Knowing they are outnumbered; they use guerilla warfare and various other types of surprise attacks to conquer and survive.

The partisan soldiers sit and talk quietly as they eat, clean guns, check ammunition. As the war presses on they all know that they will either learn through their limited training of war experience or die in the process. The absolute worst is enemy capture.

Leading this newly formed band of local rebels is a Croatian, Joseph Broz Tito. He is fifty-one, a decorated military man and revolutionary who reluctantly spent time as a political prisoner in WWI. Second in command is resistance Commander, Sephardic Jew Moshe Piade. Now aged fifty-three, he also spent time as a revolutionary and political prisoner in the same war. The youngest commander is Croatian, Stjepan Filipovic, twenty-five. He is a rising star as an ultra-loyal, home grown military player and stanch revolutionary. All three men wear light brown uniforms with their names embossed on the lapels.

"We're a small force now, but our numbers will increase as the war pushes on," Tito nods to Moshe and Stjepan as they sit together near an early morning burned out campfire. Tito's official call to rally rebel troops was via an underground Yugoslavian newspaper. He also increased his ranks by beaming the air waves of a radio station called Free Yugoslavia set up in the Soviet Union. By September of 1941, only three months later, there were approximately 200,000 partisans throughout Yugoslavia ready and more than willing to help drive out the German oppressors. Their only problem was lack of training and war munitions. They would later obtain them from the British. Unfortunately, in these early days of resistance many partisan lives were lost.

Tito became so successful at military strategy that the Germans put a dead or alive reward on his head tempting all working men with a small fortune in Reich marks. "We will move out soon." Tito motions to Stjepan.

"Yes sir." Stjepan is quick to listen and absorb.

Moshe nods and looks away with a long, drawn out stare contemplating the partisans readying themselves for the day. "We've waited a long, long time to bring these soldiers together, Tito, and suffered so much indignation and brutality from the fascists."

Tito gives Moshe a hard grimace of remembrance and nods. "Yes, and now we will fight the Germans on all fronts."

"We're all one people!" Moshe breaks out of his bitter reflection.

Stjepan jumps to his feet and commands in a loud war cry to the one hundred multiethnic soldiers waiting in the cool morning air. "Death to fascism! Freedom to the people!"

The partisan soldiers grab their rifles, raising them high in the air as an act of defiance, and a rebel yell. "Death to fascism! Freedom to the people!"

CHAPTER THREE

JANUARY, 1942, IN Yugoslavia is cold, but each person tries his best to survive. A little less than one year has passed since the German army invaded and occupied Belgrade. Growing even more insistent, their war machine expands its unrelenting hunt for Jews and Gypsies into the small surrounding towns and villages. And, hunting down humans for the Germans means turning lose their goons of choice: the collaborating Serbians, purveyors of bottomless suffering and pillagers of home, hearth and hapless families.

A small quaint town lies about thirty miles outside of Belgrade. Most of the inhabitants are friendly and mind their own business. It is New Year's Eve and Albert Jacobs, twenty-five, kisses Shayna Weinberg, eighteen. Albert is of average height, weight and olive Jewish complexion. Shayna is exceptionally beautiful with long straight brown hair. She has a youthful glow to her light skin which mimics an Aryan appearance. They both dress in conservative, but young and stylish clothes and each holds up a glass of wine as they toast to the New Year.

"Have you spoken to your parents about us yet?" Albert casually questions Shayna.

"Oh Albert," Shayna sighs. "They think I'm too young to get married. They want me to wait."

"I've waited a year now Shayna, a whole year." Albert looks at her intently.

"They know that, but with the German invasion, they just want to be cautious." Shayna says with a tilt of her head.

"Damn Germans!" Albert rattles off as if he just doesn't get it yet.

Shayna takes another drink of wine and laughs at the absurdity of it all. She remembers the traumatic events of her school days.

"Please Shayna, just talk to them again, okay?"

"Okay Albert... okay," Shayna nods her head and squints her eyes as though trying to dismiss her bad memories.

The woods in winter fall around them embracing Shayna and Albert as they walk. The glare from the packed snow blurs their vision as the cold bites their toes despite their heavy boots, but love warms their hearts. Holding hands, the world seems theirs. Albert's pupils dilate as he raises his hand to shield against the bright sun. His lips quiver as he feels a strong emotion that he can't quite yet identify. He takes a deep breath, choking it back as a ting of fright gives it up to anxiety.

The trees rise above them as birds swoop up and down, back and forth, always searching for nourishment. Albert swoons in a love trance while Shayna seems happy, yet still fumbles like a distracted young discontent. Albert studies her face as the cawing crows lift him into their world of pure nature, pure abandon. An electrical charge pulses through him as he brushes the snow off her face and puts his arm around her shoulder.

Shayna Weinberg lives in a well maintained upper middle-class household with her younger brother Walter Weinberg, eleven, and her parents who are both around forty-five years old. Murray and Bella Weinberg sit at the dining room table with their two children. The table is set with the finest of china. Gilda, a middle-aged heavy-set Jewish woman, serves them dinner.

"Thank you, Gilda," Bella smiles. "That will be all."

"Yes, Mrs. Weinberg." Gilda nods as she leaves the room.

"So, Shayna," Bella probes. "Tell your father and me again. Why do you want to marry this, Albert Jacobs?"

"Because I love him," Shayna responds abruptly while reaching for a wine glass.

Bella looks at Murray, Shayna's father, who flinches. He touches his forehead as if he had a headache. "Okay Bella, I'll speak with Albert."

"We were hoping for someone more established and with a larger income," Bella touts directly to Shayna.

"But mother, we love each other," Shayna says again.

Bella sighs. Murray stares intently at Bella who just closes her eyes in an agitated repose.

Albert and Murray sit across from each other in Murray's elegant living room. They are alone and tension fills the air. Albert is blunt and straight forward in his usual personality.

"With all due respect Mr. Weinberg, I want to marry your daughter Shayna."

There is no welcoming smile on Murray's face. "As you probably already know, for many years now, I've supported my family very well as an electrical engineer."

"Yes sir," Albert acknowledges, waiting for more.

"But Bella and I wonder can you support our daughter and a family?"

"I've been at the same bank for five years and I'm now the senior manager."

"A Jewish bank?" Murray croons the German tune.

"Yes." Albert quickly answers.

"Soon the Germans will take over the bank, confiscate the money and eliminate the Jews." Albert twists up his face in denial. "Albert, lawyers fight for the client's interest, not for the truth. Watch your inner lawyer. You know, lies that you tell yourself."

In silence, loves anticipation falls hard from Albert's face.

"I've tried to talk Bella into disappearing into Spain or going the other way into Palestine. She refuses to leave her home," Murray continues.

Albert takes a grab at ego recovery, "Shayna and I talked about maybe going to England."

"Albert, how much money do you have saved?"

Albert stares dead on at Murray as doubt returns to his face.

Shayna's middle school teacher writes the weekly essay assignment on the board. It is a most admired person project. Shayna focuses her attention on the assignment instead of on Rachel. It occurs to Shayna that her hero has to be Jesse Owens. He is the American Negro who, despite all odds and obstacles in his way, won four gold medals for himself and America by running in the 1936 Berlin Olympics. Despite the racial discrimination, Jesse actually debunked Hitler's anger and myth of Aryan supremacy in physical and mental stamina. Shayna knows from the local newspaper that Adolph Hitler had barred many Jews from competing in this Olympic Games held in Germany. Swastikas dominated everywhere. Shayna dreams to herself, *This won't stop me from hoping that someday I might do the same as my hero Jesse Owens and run in the Olympics. It might not be in Germany but in another hosting country instead.*

In the same newspaper Shayna had read that Hitler ordered all anti-Jewish signs and ethnic newspapers temporarily removed in a façade of hospitality. All this as six hundred Gypsies were registered and arrested in Berlin. They were forced by German police, under the centralized power of SS Chief Heinrich Himmler, into a concentration style camp in the East Berlin suburb of Marzahn until after the Olympics. *Cleaning up the street trash*, she recalls her fellow students' snide remarks. The lunchroom was filled with an air of their own racial superiority. *They murder all the hapless stray dogs too for no reason; I love dogs.* Shayna reflects once again upon reading an independent newspaper she found in a small Jewish grocery store near her neighborhood. It stated that sanitary conditions were inadequate in the Marzahn Camp and that Marzahn was situated near a sewage dump and cemetery. Contagious diseases spread rapidly fatally sickening many very young and older Gypsy inmates. Armed German guards stood by doing nothing to help the sick and dying.

Shayna often found the truth in the small independent newspaper which had printed that after the 1936 Olympics all Gypsies were subject to the same 1935 Nuremberg laws as the Jews. Many Gypsies who later came to the attention of the state were required to be sterilized into a non-reproductive state. Gypsy men were targeted after the Olympics and forced into slave labor in German controlled armaments plants. Their wives and children were deported and then casually disappeared into the network of newly constructed concentration camp systems.

"Isn't this a warning the Jewish people should heed?" Shayna mumbles out loud in anger. She's apprehensive at the injustice found while studying her school's archive of old newspapers and magazine. Several other students lift their heads from their books and gape at her for disturbing their concentration. Paying heed to them, Shayna continues now in quiet consternation. *Don't they get it? Wasn't Hitler just trying to dazzle foreign spectators and journalists by showing false images of a peaceful, tolerant Germany during the 1936 Olympics? At the same time, he accelerated Nazi ideology instead of telling the world of impending German aggression, or death squads for other people too.*

The next day in class, Rachel is still entranced by Ron Kaiser. She again refuses to pay attention to the teacher or even begin any of her class assignments. Shayna holds back any more reactions to her friend's waste of time thinking that she herself has more important things to do. *God save me from this love game and all this middle school drivel,* Shayna ponders. She believes herself safe for now from the Ron Kaisers, or even the Adolph Hitler's of this world. She draws into her education goals and private world of running, of future dreams and family expectations.

CHAPTER FOUR

ALBERT JACOBS IS not a pompous, pretentious man. He is a down to earth, supremely naive good guy who believes an honest man walks the toughest road. He and his parents live in a modest older middle-class family home; the furnishings are not the most stylish but it's clean and orderly. Albert's parents, Ruth and Henry Jacobs are in their early to mid-sixties, are semi-retired and live well but are not rich. Albert has an older sister, Sarah Zentall, thirty-five, who is married to Benjamin Zentall, also thirty-five. They have two children Zach, ten, and Joshua is five. Leon Jacobs, thirty, is Albert's older brother. He is married to Stella, twenty-five. With their daughter Etta, six, they are a happy family.

Albert's entire immediate family gathers at their parents' home for Sunday dinner in the dining room. Dinner is over with plates and empty wine glasses still on the table as there are no servants to carry them away. The children are in the living room playing.

Albert is beaming. "Mom, Dad, I've asked Murray Weinberg, Shayna's father for marriage."

Leon laughs. "You're going to marry Mr. Weinberg?"

"Make a cute couple," Benjamin snorts.

Albert passes them a boring glance, refusing to give them enough attention to feel noteworthy.

"Now Albert, you must complete this properly and ask for an erusin-kiddushin first," Ruth, Albert's mother, smiles.

Albert breaks it down. "Mother, there is no time for a long engagement. We must marry now because of complete German occupation soon."

"Germans? Oh Albert, I so wished that my last child would have a proper hupa kiddushin too."

"Please mother, we will have a proper marriage. Shayna and I will be leaving Yugoslavia soon, and you should too."

"Leaving? Where to? Your father and I are in our sixties now and we are tired of all this nonsense talk."

Henry Jacobs laughs. "Children, your mother lives in the past and sleeps in the present."

Ruth is adamant. "Oh Henry, I just want everything to be perfect."

"Perfect?" Henry starts to become agitated. "Nothing's perfect, nothing will ever be perfect. Wake up from your silly dreams."

"Okay that's enough." Albert steps into the middle of it. "Mother, please start planning for our wedding, now, okay?"

Ruth frowns in dejection and closes her eyes, floating somewhere between a little girl's tea party and opening birthday presents.

Albert, his mother Ruth, father Henry and his older sister Sarah sit together in the living room. Wedding plans lay in front of them on the coffee table.

Clapping her hands together with a thirst for constant applause, Ruth is ecstatic. "I've made an extensive list of wedding guests, and Rabbi Horowitz presiding."

"No mother, only immediate family members, this must be a quiet affair."

"But my dear son Albert, I want this to be a very special and elegant occasion."

Henry changes position on the sofa. "It will be Ruth, but we don't want to attract attention."

Ruth bursts out, "What about all my dear friends?"

Henry stands up. "It's dangerous to flaunt in this time of war."

Ruth pouts like the tooth fairy just forgot her, "Oh no, no, no."

Sarah interrupts. "Mother, sometimes I think that I'm the mother and that you're the child."

CHAPTER FIVE

ALBERT AND SHAYNA sit on an antique loveseat in the Weinberg living room holding hands. In front of them on the coffee table is a bottle of wine with two full wine glasses.

Shayna picks up her glass and takes a long drink. "Ah, so good, we need to celebrate." Albert picks up his glass, takes a sip and then puts the glass back down. Shayna pours more wine into both glasses.

Albert hesitates. "What, the whole bottle?"

"Maybe." Shayna picks up her glass and takes another drink. "This is so much fun."

"Yes, it is exciting, isn't it?" Albert leans over and kisses Shayna.

Shayna takes another drink of wine and laughs like she is trying to believe it all. Albert stares into her eyes with the most adoration that he can pull up, getting lost somewhere in his own head.

Standing in line for the quarter meter relay, Shayna is one of ten girls in her middle school's competition. She maneuvers line kicking her legs out like a pro, digs her sneakers into the dirt and inhales large breaths to expand her lungs. She peers nonchalantly up into the audience. Some of the eyes peering back at her are full of expectations, others saturated with dread. Still others have hope blazing in them that she will give up the race this time, letting a less trained girl come forward. *Fat chance*, Shayna reassures herself. *This is me; this is what I live for, and you can't take that away from me because it's all that I have.*

Rachel is two girls away ready to run as well, but her body isn't set and tense like Shayna's. Her mouth isn't situated into a straight tight line, her feet aren't dug in and ready to spring. Rachel glances up at the audience but seems only to flash a rush of middle school haughty ego and a smirk of happy intention knowing that everyone in the school knows her name.

Shayna turns from the audience and spreads her fingers, in front of her, readying herself for the starting pistol as she silently coaches herself. *You got to make this count, you've trained and trained, and you will fly across this track like an arrow. You will ignore the petty little middle school nonsense and be the very best that you can be.* Then the dream begins. Shayna sprouts her bird feathers and begins to soar through the white clouds and blue sky. She sees the trees below as several other large birds join her in their flight. She spreads her feathers wide open, letting the wind take her cawing like a blackbird on the wing. The smell of a new day after rain fills her nostrils with pure oxygen as she becomes weightless on the wind. She reaches out to touch a tree branch with her bird claw landing with just a wisp. The pistol goes off and 'Shayna the Bird' uses that very wispy bird claw to launch into a fiery blast off from the tree branch. She soars into the wilds of the school's solid dirt track.

I feel nothing now because my legs and feet have a mind of their own as they pump one after the other along the track. The trees and telephone poles fly by me in a fog, blending everything together. I merge with the universal bird toward the white ribbon tree approaching me. I pass the other runners who actually turn their heads to glance at me as I start to retract my wings, readying myself for the final landing. Now there is nobody on either side of me except a few beetle bugs who mistake me for a landing pad. I hear one buzzing for moisture near my pulled back open mouth and exposed teeth. I will pass the beetle bugs out of my existence as one tries to land on my head for a free sweaty ride as my arms propel me along. Now I will lift off for my finale with the beetle bug on my head. I crash past the white ribbon, breathing in steady time with the wind in my face. Hopefully it will blow the beetle bug off me. Shayna empties her thoughts as she wins the race one more time. She plants her heels in the dirt and spins in circles like a race car as she lands with her hands on her hips huffing and puffing.

Her heart is pounding like a strained steam engine. The beetle bug flies off, buzzing in a happy beetle brain fog, winning its race too in search of a mate.

Laughing out loud and smiling, Rachel is the first one by Shayna's side to pat her on the back and congratulate her. The crowd goes wild clapping and jumping with the excitement of the race, regardless of who won first place.

Bubbles blow through the air like a children's party. Shayna emerges in the full bathtub water. Candles are lit and she hums and sings softly to herself as if drowning in bliss. Walter, Shayna's younger brother, slams open the bathroom door and attempts to use the toilet.

"Please Walter, just leave. Go use the other bathroom. This is my ritual bath."

Walter purposely mangles up his face into a monster mask in the mirror. "What?"

"Yes, I'm getting married. Remember?"

Walter laughs loud and displays his Halloween monster face in full view for Shayna's reaction. "Oh, poop on you." He then leaves, slamming the door behind him.

Albert emerges in the bathtub water without candles or song. He washes as he smiles and hums to himself in pure and simple harmony.

It is early morning of the wedding day. Albert stands in the Jacobs' kitchen shoving toast in his mouth as if it would somehow calm his nerves.

Ruth enters and freezes in a forced attempt at shock. "Why are you eating on your wedding day? This is a fast day for you."

Albert immediately gulps his food like an exposed wild animal stealing food. "Oh!"

Henry walks into the kitchen and stands at attention while observing the situation with a tired yawn. "What's going on now?" Henry blinks rapidly with a heaving sigh and looks away as if bored with having to direct this circus just one more time.

"Henry, our son must follow Jewish rituals and fast on his wedding day."

"Ruth, the poor guy is nervous. Please just let him eat, okay?"

A smug look fills Ruth's face. "To be appropriate he must follow rituals." Albert chews and swallows again. "Please mother, you must stop this."

"Look Ruth," Henry flinches, "God's primary concern is not that we mindlessly follow rituals, but that we act decently."

Ruth falls into a familiar boredom, "Oh no Henry, not that again."

"Yes, dear wife, that again." Henry gives Albert a quick wink and continues with Ruth. "Ritual is only to help us become a better person, Ruth, because ethics is at Judaism's core." Ruth turns and leaves the kitchen, banging the door behind her.

Albert lets himself laugh, continuing to chew as Ruth leaves.

The Jewish synagogue is decorated for a conservative wedding as a joyous tension fills the air. Shayna dresses elegantly in a white wedding dress and Albert wears a formal dark suit and a white shirt as they both fall together in the blithering bliss of youth.

Henry Jacobs speaks to the small crowd. "Albert Jacobs has agreed with the obligations and responsibilities of a married man, to shelter and care for his wife and family."

Albert nods in agreement, "Yes."

A chuppah canopy or humppa is set up under a skylight in the synagogue roof to let the sunshine in on this joyous day. Immediate family members gather around singing Baruch Habah (Blessed is He Who Comes). Albert and Shayna approach together, coming to a stop beside each other in front of the chuppah. Albert smiles at Shayna before covering her face with a veil. He then enters the chuppah and is followed by Shayna.

Rabbi Horowitz stands across from the couple on the other side of the chuppah as he presides over the ceremony and recites a blessing over two cups of wine. "Blessed are Albert and Shayna. May they grow in their love for each other in this sacred marriage."

Rabbi Horowitz hands a glass of wine to Albert for him to take a drink. Albert then hands the glass to Shayna for her to take a drink as well. She smiles as she feels the wine going down. She laughs softly, wondering where this all will lead to. Albert then places a plain gold wedding ring on Shayna's finger. *God bless us all*, Shayna whispers to herself.

In her middle school's library Shayna reads the headlines of the most recent local newspaper announcing that on March 15, 1939, "Hitler takes Czechoslovakia." She sits down at a table to study the article then slowly lays it back down into its holder. Somehow, she feels a shadow of change falling in around her. She can't quite place it or put her finger on it from any previous experiences. She has no doubt that Hitler is moving quickly into Europe and seems to stop at nothing because no one will stop him.

Shayna shudders and leaves the library. Empty eyes, real or imagined, seem to follow her both inside and out as she walks to class. She wonders about any possible impending aggression in Yugoslavia. Most of the other students in her school are Slavic, Serbian or Croatians with a few Austrians, Italians, Germans and Greeks scattered in. *Rachel and I are the only two Jewish girls in our entire class that I'm aware of.* She focuses her attention on the obvious. *No wonder I'm feeling sick to my stomach.*

On the first day of school after summer vacation, Shayna reads the headlines of her library's most recent local newspaper. It announces that on September 1, 1939, "Hitler takes Poland." Several days later the same newspaper's headline announces: "Britain and France declare war on Germany." *Someone's finally going to stop Hitler,* Shayna cheers to herself. She lingers on the front page a little too long. Other students impatiently stand in line behind her waiting to read the latest war stories too. She likes that other countries are now fighting Hitler and thinks, *Maybe this German hostility will all be over soon, and things can get back to normal.*

The following day Shayna is in the library again, standing at attention as she reads the latest articles about the German onslaught and invasion. " Blitzkrieg," Shayna interprets from the article is what the German's call their style of dominance and take over as they attack a small section of a target country and then proceed aggressively through the rest of the country with intimidation and terror. Shayna stops reading for a moment to digest this new threat. A wall clock screeches out its coo-coo bird hour. Shayna watches as it finishes its cold-call and then pulls back into its safe clock haven until the next hour's job. Feeling nauseas, Shayna returns to the article. It goes on saying that this style of belligerence is dependent upon surprise attacks, unpreparedness and most of all swift German assaults with little or no regard for the inhabitants. She continues reading and then stops in horror, staring at the blank wall in front of her as if having a vision of things to come.

"Are you done with the paper now?" Ron Kaiser interrupts her trance as he forcefully grabs the newspaper out of Shayna's hands. "Rachel told me what you said about me being an egotistical ass-hole!"

Shayna breaks from the wall, jumping up and jangling in surprise as if the enemy were finally stalking her. For just a shattered instant she searches Ron's face. There is nothing there but contorted revulsion for her, locked in an image of frightening self-importance. *You're a legend in your own mind,* Shayna wants to spit out at him in vengeance. She stands her ground, holding it in for another day. Instead she backs off, saying absolutely nothing, knowing that it would only make matters worse.

Disdainfully, Ron grips the newspaper with a furious intensity. He stomps away toward a table and then halts in his tracks. He turns around sneering at Shayna, "Go run in the traffic, a German tank is waiting for you."

CHAPTER SIX

WARM AND COZY is the feeling on this cold winter evening inside the small reception room attached to the synagogue. A small group of three musicians play the Jewish wedding song, 'Siman Tov u'Mazal Tov.' Albert and Shayna sit at the front table while their immediate family members sit directly behind them at other tables. Bella sits in a middle chair between Murray and Walter who wears a tie, a fitted suit and displays a pompous smirk.

"Where's the food?" Walter demands. "I'm hungry."

Bella chides him. "Walter, please be quiet. The food will be served soon."

Walter pouts and crosses his hands over his chest in an act of defiance. Murray gets up from his chair, changes places with Bella and sits down directly beside Walter. Walter steals a look up at Murray and then scowls away, now somewhat defeated in his plans to terrorize Shayna's wedding. *Walter acts angry all the time now.* Murray squints and wonders just what damages have been done to Walter by his classmates.

Ruth beams in complete adoration and joy. "What a wonderful wedding reception, and the music is so very pleasant."

Bella smiles back at Ruth. Murray looks away nervously as if expecting something.

"Let's eat now Ruth, please." Henry looks around somewhat apprehensive as if not knowing just what to expect from the evening either.

Ruth floats on endless wings toward the covered dishes and uncovers them. "Everyone, please help yourself to the many blessings of this wonderful food."

Gilda, Bella's maid, steps up to the serving table and pours glasses of wine. The guests help themselves to the wine, waiting patiently as Gilda hands each a plate of food. Guests mill around and talk pleasantries then sit down at their tables to enjoy friends and family.

Rabbi Horowitz thanks the wedding party and then leaves somewhat abruptly. The three musicians are playing the song, 'Hava Nagillah' and most guests engage in a small hora or circle dance. Albert and Shayna stand up, bow to each other, then prance toward the dance floor. They are frolicking in their love. It is a moment of total contentment.

"It's all so wonderful." Ruth exhilarates as she motions Murray to the dance floor.

Murray shakes his head no, refusing to dance. He continues to agonize and fret as a strange anxiousness begins to take its toll on his enjoyment of the evening. Bella notices Murray's uneasiness and takes a seat next to him and Henry.

Murray alternatively pounds his fingers on the table. "Some people are leaving Yugoslavia on bicycles with nothing, just to escape the Germans."

Henry nods. "It's really frightening."

Bella is absorbed. "Let's close this down and go home."

Murray looks at her intently. "Yes, I think so too. What about you Henry?"

"Yes, go ahead Bella, thank our guests and say goodnight."

Bella stands up and approaches the three musicians who are taking a break. She whispers something to them and hands them their money, then addresses the guests. "Thank you to the fabulous musicians and to everyone for all the blessings. God go with you and goodnight."

Everyone smiles and claps softly except Ruth. She runs forward waving her hands like a traffic cop. "Bella, why is it over so soon, so early... why?"

"Thank you so much Ruth for all your perfect wedding planning. It's a great success." Bella remains kind but firm.

Ruth stutters and fumbles. "Yes, and thank you... but... but the evening's still young."

Bella takes Ruth's hand. "We all appreciate you so much, Ruth."

Ruth drops Bella's hand, almost shoving it away and then slowly ambles off. Bella walks back to her chair and sits down again with Murray and Henry.

Sarah Zentall stands up and comforts her mother Ruth with a hug, like reassuring a sulking little girl. "Mother, the wedding is perfect just like you wanted, but we all must go now... please."

"Why Sarah, rush, rush, rush?"

The musicians pack up their instruments as Albert stands up and addresses everyone. "Thanks to all for the wedding gifts, bless you all and goodnight."

As the musicians are leaving, Bella and Gilda stand beside the door. Bella hands Gilda payment for her services, "Thank you Gilda, you did a wonderful job." Gilda gives a nod of thanks and exits into the night.

Murray stands up. "Thanks to everyone, but we must leave now. The wedding is over. Bless you all and goodnight." Murray is unyielding, *Why don't they just go?*

Ruth interrupts again. "Hurry, hurry, hurry, I thought that this was a happy wedding." Everyone just stares at Murray with questions lingering in their eyes.

"Go now. Just go! Please!" Murray demands as irritation spreads onto his face.

Shayna sits by herself in the school cafeteria eating her paper bag lunch. As Rachael approaches with her lunch tray, Shayna looks away. Rachel hesitates briefly, recognizing something is wrong, but sits down at the same table anyway.

"Hi, Shayna," Rachel squeaks out waiting for acknowledgement.

"Hi," Shayna remarks without emotion.

"What's wrong with you?" Rachel questions. She conceals her suspicions with an easy-going smile followed by a carefree laugh.

Shayna remains silent as she continues chewing her food in thought.

"Well, what's on your mind?" Rachel feigns indifference. She reads Shayna's nonverbal body language and it appears to sink in that maybe she let her gossipy tongue slip a little bit too much. Rachel wonders if her boyfriend, Ron Kaiser, has finally confronted Shayna.

"Nothing or nobody really important," Shayna almost pouts wanting to stand up and leave.

Rachel is uncertain but continues, "Okay then, I want to ask your opinion about something."

"Oh yeah, Rachel. What is it about this time, some crazy boy?"

Rachel lowers her head pursing her lips tight together as if trying to shut something out. Tears start to stream down as she lets it come out fast. "Ron called me a bitch and said that he can't see me anymore because I'm a Jew and he's a German. His family says that our relationship is forbidden by law."

Shayna is stunned into silence. Rachel watches Shayna's pupils dilate as her mouth drops into an anxious frown. Shayna contemplates Rachel's words as if the hurricane has finally arrived. Shayna places her sandwich onto the brown paper sack saying nothing. She continues to hold her frown as her head rings in a foreboding alarm.

CHAPTER SEVEN

EVERYONE PREPARES TO leave, but there is a loud knock on the reception room side door. Any small talk cuts short as undivided attention focuses on the closed door. The loud knocking continues.

All eyes turn to Murray for his reaction. "Don't answer it. Just be quiet." Knowing it's not friendly Murray gives a hand signal for silence. The entire group stands in bewilderment.

The loud knocking turns into an even louder banging followed by an angry command. "Open the door now or we'll break it down! That's an order!"

All are speechless and frozen. The loud banging turns into angry kicks against the door and a piercing authority. "Last warning, open now or the door will be broken down!"

Murray pauses, remembering with regret his forewarning of anxiety. The door squeaks as he opens it slowly, not wanting to let in the devil that is waiting outside. There it stood, not one devil but four Belgrade special police officers. Their arrogance is more than obvious as they stand outside the door in dark uniforms, heavy boots and billed hats.

Murray gawks at them, suspended in disbelief as his fears have finally materialized. The officers watch him with cold, hard glares. Murray takes a deep breath and slowly releases it. "Yes, what can I do for you, officers?" Murray hangs onto his composure despite the urge to attack. Having no firearms and family in tow, he decides it is best to remain peaceable.

The first officer steps forward. "A report has been made that Jews are disturbing the peace."

Murray stays polite. "There is no noise coming from this synagogue; it's a quiet wedding."

The officer continues ignoring Murray's truth. "Nevertheless, we have orders to arrest everyone here."

"No, that's not necessary. We will disperse now, immediately. The wedding is over anyway." The officer just gawks at Murray blank faced holding his macho.

"Let's go, everyone." Murray gives a friendly laugh and begins to help the guests exit. The guests begin to leave out the door behind Murray.

The first commanding officer shakes his head no and blocks the doorway with his heavy boot and a nightstick.

"My family has done nothing, just take me. I will go, just take me." Murray acquiesces.

Benjamin Zentall comes forward. "Take me too. Please just let my family go. They have done nothing."

Leon Jacobs now comes forward. "I'll go. Just take me." Albert walks forward. "I'll go with them too."

The officer snickers. "Everyone must go. You are all under arrest. Women and children included."

"What?" Albert gasps in an unsettling shock, unsure of what to do next. Suddenly Ruth falls on a table and wine glasses crash to the floor.

"Order! Order!" The officer demands. "Leave everything except your coats and get in line. Now! Now!"

Everyone is frozen in disbelief. Not sure of what to do, they do nothing.

The second officer barks, "The Government of National Salvation in the Territory of the German Army Military Occupation and Commander in Serbia orders your arrests for disturbing the peace."

Ruth Jacobs stands up from the tabletop and cries out amid the broken glass. "No, no, I won't go with you. I'm going home to my house that I've lived in for forty years. I won't go to jail! For what? For what? I have done nothing illegal!"

As the last two officers step forward, the first officer gives them orders. "Take this woman outside, now."

Ruth screams even louder. "No, No. I won't go. No!"

The officers grab Ruth by the arms and drag her toward the door. Ruth fights and screams. "Get your hands off me. I'm innocent."

Henry rushes toward the door, trying to forcefully take back his wife. "Please don't take my wife. She's getting older and sometimes acts like a child again. Please!"

The fourth officer pushes Henry to the floor fighting and clawing to get up, but he is held down and gagged. The second officer pulls his gun on Albert and the other men, threatening them if they try to intervene. A gnawing terror takes over everyone's faces.

"Grandma... Grandma!" Walter screams.

Bella grabs Walter and covers his mouth. Sarah and Stella both grab their children and pull them close, hiding their faces with their skirts. Through all of this the children are scared and crying.

With tears flowing, Stella calls out "Oh, my dear God, please help us!"

Sarah pleads with the children. "Children please try to be quiet. These are dangerous men!"

Henry breaks free from the floor, throws off his gag, pushes through the officers and runs outside to rescue his wife Ruth.

A loud gunshot is heard.

Henry stops abruptly when he sees Ruth's body in a heap in front of the synagogue. He rushes over to her and falls to his knees, "Ruth, Ruth... Oh My God... No! No!"

CHAPTER EIGHT

STILL WEARING HER wedding dress, Shayna stares out from behind the prison bars at the Belgrade Police Station. Her entire family is in one cell while Albert and his entire family are confined in another cell. All the children whine and cry as Stella and Sarah do their best to calm them.

Enjoying a sandwich, one of the guards shouts out in stony callousness. "Shut those brats up now or there will be consequences!"

Both families are grouped on the outside planks of the Belgrade station as they wait for transport trucks to arrive. All are still dressed in their wedding attire from the previous night's reception. Albert's white shirt under his black suit coat is now stained with dirt, and his hair is matted with sweat. Bits of Shayna's wedding dress trail behind when she walks. Looking like pieces of holiness deserting her, the ripped white lace is a silent clue of what lies ahead.

In total there are about two hundred people waiting. All are being held against their will under armed guard for no apparent reason. The group consists of other Jewish families, ethnic civilian Serbians and Slavic peasant farmers. All are frightened and stand together in family groups. Standing slightly from the main group are four mixed ethnic Yugoslav partisan war rebels. They are wearing combinations of light brown military uniforms and street clothes.

Albert and Murray sit together talking. Albert turns his head slowly, taking them all in. "I had no idea that so many ethnic Slavic and Serbian people would be here with us."

Murray nods knowing now they have all entered a nightmare. "So, the Germans want the Slavs gone too?"

"Oh yeah," Murray affirms. "Without collaborators from within like the corrupt Serbian bureaucrats and local police, the Germans wouldn't be so strong."

"What exactly do they want?" Albert looks puzzled.

"Germany wants lots of land and lots of money." Murray says with a grimace.

"So, this is why they target the Jews?"

"Exactly, they need money for their war machine and many Jews have money." Albert narrows his eyes absorbing the immoral concept.

Murray continues holding back his anger for his family's sake. "The Germans think that they will go on for the next twenty years, expanding everywhere."

A Serbian guard approaches them in a dark military uniform, clanking his heels as he nears. "But," Albert looks up and sees the guard coming.

The Serbian guard's heavy boots stomp the ground in front of them. "No political conversations, no loud talk, no writing, no singing, or you will be executed immediately!"

Four large open military trucks pull up. All two hundred people load like cattle onto the trucks with approximately fifty to each truck. Many women and children cry and moan. The Serbian State guards have no mercy. Some Jewish men and Slavic peasant farmers are beaten and kicked as they resist getting on the trucks.

It's a wet snowy morning as Shayna waits for the school bus to pick her up. She pulls the knitted hat, a childhood birthday present from her now deceased grandmother, further down over her face. The cold air makes her shiver and the snowflakes melt on her nose, dripping down into her mouth. For some peculiar reason the snowy water tastes bitter now as never before and she spews it out onto the street instead of swallowing it as usual. *When I was a kid, I always loved snow falling and ice skating and snow sledding, but now everything about winter seems cold and menacing.* She reflects to herself. *Has the world changed, or is it just me?*

As the bus pulls up Shayna shakes the snow and water off her coat imitating the wet animals in the zoo. She pauses a few seconds to stomp her boots before getting onto the bus. The regular bus driver is indifferent to her as usual, but all her classmates' eyes follow her every move as she feels them bearing down on her in some sort of personal judgment. There are a few open seats and she searches the other students' faces for a friendly smile inviting her to sit with them, but everyone looks away and pretends that they don't see her. She grabs the middle pole for balance as the bus takes off shaking and pulling in the frozen slush. Considering her numb feet and hands she tries to ignore the pain but navigates to a resting place for safety.

Shayna sees an open seat next to one of the girls in her second period math class and without another thought sits down next to her. This Ukrainian girl, who always seemed friendly and often asked Shayna for advice about running, won't even look at her now. She displays agitation that Shayna has the nerve to even sit down next to her. Shayna feels the eyes around her digging holes into her skin as she conceals the anxiety surging through her body. She lowers her head as vulnerability takes over her once happy being with a deep, distressing emptiness. She wonders just what it is that she has done or said to deserve this harsh and cruel punishment from her once responsive fellow classmates. *When I was younger, I always looked forward to going to school and learning. Now it seems to be just another annoying chore like taking out the trash,* she reminisces as disappointment floods her mind.

There is a seat open two benches away next to another girl that Shayna occasionally sits with at lunch when Rachel isn't at school. She gets up and goes to sit with her part-time lunchroom friend letting the girl from the Ukraine sit alone in her mean little world. "Hi," Shayna reaches out to her cafeteria friend, but the girl turns her head in silence refusing to make eye contact. Instead she just gazes out of the school bus window without a welcoming gesture or pleasant word to Shayna. Someone in the back of the bus starts laughing in a shrill, sharp tone that sends a chill of fear through Shayna. Shayna withdraws into herself as her stomach tightens into a knot. For a quick minute she almost feels like vomiting up her breakfast. She knows now that she is on the bus with her follow classmates surrounding her, yet she is alone in her empty heart and in the silence that fills the once rambunctious fun bus. Appearing to her now as she closes her eyes and waits for the ride to end is the image of a former school bus rider who was also humiliated off by bullies. He was a fragile special education student who had a learning disability and stuttered. She now remembers him with heartbreak and pity as never before.

The school bus finally arrives at the school and lets the students get off, but Shayna sits until everyone else leaves to regain her shaken composure and wounded sense of pride. She stands up and then trails out of the bus dragging her feet and wearing a fixed confused stare. Tears were trying to fall but she choked them back. All she wanted to do now was go back home. When she nears her locker to put her wet jacket and scarf away, she sees a white note taped to the outside of it. She approaches in trepidation, takes the note in her hand, and begins to read it: GO HOME JEW is printed in red pencil as if someone in school authority had given the order.

Shayna's first period class is no different. When she walks into the room her normal desk has been pushed away and separated from the others as if she had a contagious disease.

"What's going on?" The teacher calls out to the other students. "Who moved Shayna's chair like this?" The teacher moves Shayna's desk to its normal place in the group, but when Shayna goes to the restroom and comes back her chair has again been separated from the others. However, this time it is turned toward the wall so that there is absolutely no doubt that the other students do not want her in the classroom with them.

CHAPTER NINE

SOMEWHERE IN THE mountains of Yugoslavia the multiethnic rebel partisans move to a new camp. As they settle in around mid-day Stjepan Filipovic runs toward Josip Broz Tito and Moshe Piade as they unload their gear. "A German reconnaissance unit has been spotted," Stjepan blurts out.

Tito and Moshe glare at each other as a chill of adrenalin flushes on their faces. Tito picks up his rifle. "They must be stopped!"

In contained excitement Moshe gives the order. "We will quietly move out, now." All three men salute each other.

Eight German SS police driving four kubelwagens pull up to a Slavic peasant farmer at work in his field. The Germans are dressed in dark uniforms, dark boots, billed hats and wear swastika arm bands. The commanding SS officer in the lead kubelwagen exits, slamming the door behind him as if the farmer were in fact trespassing on his personal property. The farmer looks up, squinting in disbelief as the SS officer approaches him.

The SS officer gives the Nazi salute to the farmer as he nears. "The Government of National Salvation in the Territory of German Military Occupation and Commander in Serbia orders confiscation of this land."

The farmer's mouth gapes open. "This land has been in my family for generations. It's not yours to take."

"You and your family will be off this land within one week or the German military will escort you and your family to a concentration camp."

The farmer draws up his face incensed. "Leave now bullies! Get off my land!"

"This land is for German population expansion. Slavs don't

deserve it; Slavs don't deserve to live, at all."

"I will not leave! Take you swastika arm bands and get out! Get out! Now!"

The SS officer pulls out a rifle and shoots it into the air. The Slavic farmer backs down and immediately rushes away, frightened but not intimidated.

The SS officer gets back into his kubelwagen and all four vehicles drive away from the farm and the Slavic villages along the deserted dirt roads of the back woods. They head toward the Belgrade area where they are secretly headquartered.

Fifty armed Yugoslav rebels hide in the brush and trees along the same deserted road, waiting for the German SS police. The four kubelwagens slowly make their way up the road. The Germans are armed and attentive as they pass in front of the hidden fifty-armed Yugoslav partisans.

The partisans shoot at the Germans from cover of the trees and brush. Rifle blasts pound away for about a minute. All the German officers either tumble out of the kubelwagens to the ground, or slump into their seats in a pile of lifelessness. Emerging from the brush, the partisans check all of the Germans to confirm they're dead and then collect the weapons and other useful military equipment. Once done, they drag the bodies out of the kubelwagens and hide them in the brush and trees.

The rebels then jump into the kubelwagens. One young partisan holds up a machine gun and ammunition he discovered hidden under a mat on the floor of the kubelwagen. The other partisans search their vehicles and wave confiscated weapons in the air. There is a loud roar of victory and the newly acquired kubelwagens full of rebels drive down the dirt road, returning to the forest proud of their victory over the fascists.

Ten Yugoslav partisans stand guard as others dig trenches in the forest. Those digging throw in all eight naked bodies of the dead SS police officers. The German uniforms are piled near the grave site like used tin cans.

Shayna stays to herself more than ever for the remainder of high school knowing that her classmates hate her because she's a

Jew. She has not accepted their hatred, but keeps convincing her-self, *I must finish out my senior year and graduate so that I can eventually get into college. I will not let these nasty little immature brats destroy my life.* She sees Rachel occasionally in school, but Rachel is considering dropping out because of all the hateful notes and judgments against her. She tells Shayna that she just can't take much more. Her ex-boyfriend, Ron Kaiser, has a new Russian girlfriend and he has been ignoring Rachel for a long time now. As usual, he concentrates only on his own importance as the school's soccer star. Rachel is now alone most of the time, sitting by herself at lunch just like Shayna. Shayna doesn't speak to anyone except her teachers but is becoming more accustomed to seclusion as she has always been a loner. However, she notices the pressure on Rachel is wearing her down. It seems way too heavy for her low self-esteem and shaky self-image to handle.

In the last month of their senior year, eight female runners are poised and ready for their final competition. It will end the racing season with a send-off for most of the students to advance into their dream colleges next year. Shayna hasn't started to apply to colleges yet. It is an enormous challenge to just show up every day and try to function as a normal student. She tries to ignore the vicious gazes and hostility toward her, but it is wearing thin on her too. She is near bursting with indignation, many times wanting to scream back insults at the bullying students. Instead, she chokes out her personal stress as a cold's mucous many times onto the ground. She somehow maintains her burning composure, except when physically threatened. In the back of her mind, her main goal is to graduate, and maybe having the joy of racing just one more time. She has given up on early morning runs on the school track because of constant harassment and depression, but she still runs through her neighborhood and the nearby park on weekends. Her family knows about the discrimination and revulsion against her at school. They stand firmly behind her in finishing out the school year and being strong in the face of conflict and opposition. Avoiding the bus, Shayna's mother Bella drives her to school each morning and picks her up afterwards and she does the same with Shayna's younger brother Walter. His school mates express their ugly loathing and aversion toward him too. In contrast, he dares to make faces back at them and insult them in equal terms with scathing imitations. He stands in their faces with malicious racial and religious slurs of his own. He survives their degradation by scoffing at the whole thing as middle school chaos and just plain stupidity.

Walter has reported them to the school counselors and principal many times, but nothing much is ever done about it. Receiving no punishment or counseling for their cruel and unusual behavior, the bully boy gang continues. Now they are even more relentless with their escalating spitefulness toward Walter. When the bullies gang up on him now, Walter has learned to survive with equivalent insanity. He threatens them with such viciousness that they are intimidated as he stands alone. He uses his own simulation of his favorite comic book monster and backs them down with a distorted, screwed up face and a loud, crazed monster howl. All the while he holds an open toothed mouth ready to bite at the first touch. Seeing all this they disperse and run away like scared little girls. Alternating a warped smirk and an indignant smile, Walter revels in his notorious reputation as the 'crazy Jew bastard'. *If the principal can't protect me, then I will protect myself,* Walter rationalizes. He stands in his first period class with brows lifted over piercing alligator eyes, flashing his burning teeth and clenched fists as anger quivers on his lips.

CHAPTER TEN

FOUR LARGE OPEN military trucks full of multi-ethnic prisoners arrive at the gate. A sign posted at the entrance reads: ANHALTELEGER DEDINJE (Banjica Concentration Camp). It is the former 18th Infantry Army Barracks of the Royal Yugoslav Army, Belgrade Yugoslavia. Banjica is a smaller camp and can hold approximately two thousand to a maximum of three thousand prisoners at a time. It was originally intended for Serbian Communists, Slavic peasant farmers and Royalists who resisted the occupation of the Regime. It was destined to house Jewish and Gypsy inmates as well.

The gate opens and allows the trucks to drive through. It's a cold day and all prisoners exit the trucks wearing some sort of coat. They are all dirty and worn down. The old and sick limp along while working to hold each other up. Murray, Bella and Albert gather their two families. They stand side by side, women holding close to their children and the men guarding around them. Several Serbian State guards approach the prisoners whose terrified faces wonder what is to come next.

The commanding Serbian guard, nicknamed Jingo, speaks first. "Attention listen up now! Men will move to the right, women and children to the left." The prisoners respond in accordance to his command in cold fear and silence. "All nationalities of partisan rebels will be processed first and will be put into the separate barracks number four, number four."

The partisan prisoners glower at Jingo in hate. He ignores them.

"The rebels will now go up the steps," Jingo points up, "and straight into the main room. You will be processed and identified there now! Move!"

The Yugoslav partisans cautiously move up the steps shooting back visual arrows at Jingo. He dismisses their fear and suffering with a contemptuous smirk.

"When the rebels are finished, civilian men will proceed up the stairs next. Understood?"

The women shiver and huddle closer together with their children for warmth. Albert considers the women. "Can't the women and children go next, ah, ah, sir?"

"Silence!" Jingo screams at Albert. Albert contorts his face in revulsion.

The second ranking guard walks over to Albert and points a rifle in his face. Albert grimaces and looks away with controlled but subverted anger.

"After processing, civilian men will go into men's barracks number three. Woman and children will go into women's barracks number two. Got that? Men three, women two."

Albert stares at Jingo in disgust, but Jingo ignores him again. As the two hundred prisoners gawk at Jingo, the setting sun casts a long shadow making him seem taller, fiercer and larger than life itself.

There are approximately one hundred women and children of different ethnicities in barracks number two, including the new arrivals from the Belgrade area. Each barracks has smaller cells or large bedrooms in them for several women at a time. The toilets and washrooms are in a common area. There is barely any heat in the entire women's barracks and each wooden bed has only two wool army blankets on it.

An older, seemingly unsentimental Jewish woman in an iron grey dress is the barrack's leader and her name is Ester. She gives each new prisoner a camp uniform of drab pants and shirt to wear.

Stella Jacobs frowns in contempt at Ester. "Is there hot water in the showers?"

"Just warm," Ester replies curtly.

In agitation Stella looks away.

Speaking like a robot in a drab monotone, Ester shuffles her feet, dragging herself along. "This cell unit works the laundry for cleaning camp clothing and bed sheets. All children will stay here while you work."

"But, will the children be alright while we're gone?" Stella remarks in high pitched anxiety.

Ester withholds her response momentarily to quiet Stella's frustration. "I will choose two women to watch all the children each day. You will rotate."

A snarl pulls up Stella's face. "Why are you doing this? You are Jewish too, right?"

"Who would you prefer to be your barrack's leader, a German woman?"

Stella's face drops, releasing her pent-up tears as she collapses onto the bed. "Dear God, please help us, please."

"I'm a prisoner too," the barracks leader remarks. "If you have any jewelry on, hide it now." Shayna glances at her wedding ring.

There are approximately one hundred men of different ethnicities in barracks number three including the new arrivals from the Belgrade area. This barracks also has small cells or bedrooms for several men, but it's furnished with more blankets than the woman's barracks and there is heat to preserve the male labor force. Murray's group is given one cell for all in their group containing several single beds. Murray, Benjamin, Leon, Henry and Albert all undress for the showers. An older Jewish man, Aaron, is their barrack's leader and they are also given uniforms of drab pants and shirts to wear.

Aaron addresses the group. "Each of you will be given a different work assignment according to your training and education."

Albert's eyebrows twitch at him.

"Those of you without a vocation will dig ditches and empty the latrines."

"What's the point?" Albert jeers.

Aaron continues, ignoring Albert's comment. "You will be assigned tasks to help the Germans further their goals."

"Yes sir, glad to help the Germans get ahead." Albert sneers.

Aaron just looks at Albert with sad, broken eyes.

As Shayna readies herself for her last running match, she digs her sneaker into the dirt for a swift take off. A fly lands on the hairs of her arm and she twitches with an itch that she longs to scratch. She doesn't want to move now because she has readied herself mentally for the starting shot to go off. As she peers down at the fly, it rubs its front legs together readying itself also for a planned take off using Shayna's arm as its launch pad and appears content with life in its own little flying endeavors. Everything has changed now. *Racing competition doesn't thrill me so much anymore as when I was younger, and it was fun. Now I feel like I'm just going through the motions of habit and circumstance. I miss the contented days of my childhood when everyone liked me at school and I had the freedom to be myself without feeling anger, resentment, sorrow,* she recalls going back to those carefree days just like the blissful fly on her arm. *But that is impossible,* Shayna is well aware as she floats off momentarily. She glances again sideways at the fly and somehow envies its freedom and indifference to a cold, cruel world. All it has to do is find some dog poop and then buzz away again for a couple of days in cheerful fly ignorance. "No brain, no pain," she drifts out loud shrugging and shaking her itching arm. The fly hesitates for another second and then makes its racing getaway, continuing on its own life's journey to find other flies, mate and have maggots just like she remembers learning about in biology class. Shayna breaths out to the fly, "Good luck with your dreams," she watches it go thinking, *be careful little buddy, you only have three worries: fly paper, a swatter... a spider.*

That's what I'm facing, Shayna suddenly feels the need to shout out to the audience. However, they have neither understanding nor really want to be bothered or care if she is in dire emotional pain and can't find a way to break out of the fly paper. When she glances up into the audience all she sees now are bones, skeletons draped in human clothes and moving skulls like the handmade dolls for sale in the Yugoslavian farmer's market, inanimate objects with no minds of their own or maybe they're just big spiders waiting for her to get caught up in their tangled web.

It's night and the women's barracks temperature hangs below the freezing point. Many women are two or three to a small bed, huddled together in their coats for warmth. Each woman has only one blanket to keep or share with their children.

Bella huddles with Walter. With beds pushed together and curled up beside them are Stella and her young daughter Etta. In the next bed Sarah Zentall clenches her two young boys all with heads under the blanket. Their foggy breath rises in the cold night air.

Between them all is Shayna who cries softly to herself. She tries to curl up under the ends of everyone's blankets. *What happened to me?* She wonders as her mind drifts between sliding, intermittent tears. *Just yesterday I was the most popular athlete in school. How did I end up like this? My adult life has just begun and now I'm in prison.* Her tears fall faster and harder now, freezing on her face. Shayna's white wedding dress lies peeking out of a nearby trash can.

It's night in the men's barracks. The heat is on and the men relax in semi-comfort. Albert lies on his bed and stares up at the shifting ceiling shadows. The thoughts of the last few days shift quickly and randomly through his head. *I remember Murray warning me of this very nightmare and now it has come to pass. How could I have not listened to him and left Yugoslavia earlier? Now we are all hoarded like insects into some crazy roach trap awaiting destruction of the useless.*

CHAPTER ELEVEN

THE NEXT DAY all civilian male prisoners line up in the main courtyard in front of two portable tables. Multiple armed Serbian guards surround about one hundred civilian men, but the rebels are not present. A Serbian guard sits at each table. Each has a clipboard with names of the civilian men as they were registered upon arrival. The third and fourth guards have their rifles ready.

The first guard motions for men to come to his table, each in their turn. "Each worker will be issued a personal identification card with your race stamped on it."

"What does my race have to do with anything?" Albert mumbles to himself.

The guard stares blankly at him. "Next."

Albert walks up to the table.

"Name."

"Albert Jacobs," he utters. His eyes fall cold and distant seemingly beaten.

"Occupation?"

"Bank manager."

"How long?"

"Five years."

"Move back to your barracks... Next."

Albert silently jeers at the guard in annoyance. *You little piece of shit*, Albert thinks. *How dare you treat us this way.*

"Next, I said." The guard glares up at Albert, willing him to leave immediately.

Maybe I should just punch your stupid face right now, Albert considers his choices.

Murray steps forward and lightly pushes Albert out of the way, "Murray Weinberg."

Albert backs off, dragging his feet out from under his body step by step.

"Occupation?"

"Electrical engineer."

"How long?"

"Twenty years."

"Move back to your barracks."

Murray steps back and lets the next man through.

Returning from her insect reverie, Shayna shakes the spider web images out of her head and tightens her body again for the starting pistol. Suddenly an empty glass bottle flies though the air just missing her head and crashes at her feet. "What?" Shayna yells as her own anger finally flies out as well. "What's this?" As she looks around to see where the bottle could have come from, she hears a most scathing male voice screeching from the audience, "Dirty Jew! Go take a bath! You stink!"

Shayna shuts her eyes tight holding back the tears. She swallows down the pain, hiding it inside of herself, as her own personal skeleton image of the audience once more falls vividly in her mind's eye. Even more horrible, the skeletons are now replete with carnivorous teeth, ripping and tearing down on her as if their hot breath was scorching and shredding her very being.

Shayna opens her eyes and glances down at Rachel who is two girls away; Rachel seems totally oblivious to the bottle incident as if it never happened. *After all the bottle didn't land at Rachel's feet but at mine,* Shayna considers cringing as her neck muscles tighten up into a worthless painful knot. "I'm running backwards now," she says out loud knowing the most important thing in her life is suddenly fading away from her just out of reach, just out of touch.

They have finally taken away all of my happiness and desire to run. They are trying to destroy me. She totally understands this now in a newfound silent consciousness.

With a sudden flash, the sun disappears behind the clouds and a light mist of rain blows, moistening the tense air as if just ordered by an unseen hand to cool things off. Shayna hears the pistol to start the race, but intentionally ignores it and stands frozen in her tracks. She continues to hold her most professional starting position like a lifeless department store mannequin. Rachel runs on as if a spider is chasing her as she carries her Jewish self, unscathed by any thrown bottle.

Finally relaxing and assuming a spectator's stance, Shayna regrets losing out on the race, but wills Rachel to run forward in her place. On and on Rachel flees with the mist in her face.

Maybe she's afraid that another bottle will come out of nowhere and hit her in the head, she's running faster than she has ever run before. She is amazing. Shayna recalls remembering the casual indifference and slow pace of Rachel's usual racing. There is absolutely no comparison to what she sees her do today in this very race and on this very track. She is beyond amazing. Shayna smiles up to the sky and lets the rain brush her face like tears.

Shayna stands firm, watching as Rachel bursts through the white ribbon first, many yards ahead of any of the other girls. Instead of stopping for the enthusiastic excitement of the winner's circle, Rachel just keeps on running, running further around the entire track and eventually coming back toward the white ribbon finish line. *She seems to be a windup toy or a time clock that just won't stop ticking,* and Shayna has a feeling that she knows why. As Rachel returns to the winner's circle there are petty quarrels and heated arguments all around her and several of the other racers try to slap Rachel in the face. The same coach that Shayna had turned down for the cheerleading position now comes forward and hesitantly pats Rachel on the back. It's as if she's giving Rachel a consolation prize of attention before hitting her with bad news.

Over the loudspeaker Shayna hears: *"There has been a foul."* She simpers to herself knowing that Rachel is in for heartache. The voice over the loudspeaker continues, *"Rachel Cohen has been disqualified and Karen Kaiser is declared the winner."* Rachel freezes and looks up at the loudspeaker, then over to the coach to confirm or reject this accusation.

"But what did I do wrong?" Rachel pleads disarmingly to the female coach.

"You started too soon." The stone-faced coach spits out to Rachel without a flinch as she blows her shrill whistle and raises her hands. "Rachel ran before the starting shot," the coach proclaims clearing her throat and silencing the quarreling girls as her face draws up into a hard, cruel mask. Shayna, *horrified by now,* has never seen this look before in her entire time at school. Shayna gawks a long time at the coach wondering who this new emerging mean person is, and where she came from.

This same disqualifying excuse is announced over the loudspeaker again just for absolute confirmation for the watching assembly. The crowd goes wild cheering for Karen Kaiser, Ron's younger sister, who now parades herself about. She gives herself a frenzied clapping session and pats herself on the back as the other five runners mob her. They are keeping face with affection and applause and most of all making sure that they are not labeled sore losers.

"No, Rachel did not start too soon," Shayna broadcasts out loud to the crowd and is positive of this with a head shaking affirmation. "I was watching Rachel the entire time after the glass bottle landed to see if Rachel was going to run." No one pays attention to Shayna much less cares what she has to say anymore. *It's just like the 1936 Olympics when Hitler was in the grandstands.* Shayna argues with only herself, *no Jews allowed.*

Karen Kaiser now prances out into center field and raises her arms into the air like 'Queen for the Day' taking charge of her subjects as if the world has inevitably fallen at her feet. Her long straight, wet blond hair sticks to her head in the rainy misty. She shakes it off and poses her best side forward with a perfect white toothed grin, posing for the finest picture of her first racing debut photo in the school's newspaper. Rachel stands by speechless, dressed in an air of utter disbelief and desperately aware that the foul was concocted and unjustified. She is now and finally on trial for being a Jew.

Rachel haphazardly stumbles across the track toward Shayna who by now has kicked the glass bottle out of her way. Shayna is ambling back toward the dressing room. Rachel follows Shayna with her eyes focused in obvious pain. Her nostrils are flaring, and her teeth are clenched, causing her jaw to protrude forward, one part furious and one part proud.

CHAPTER TWELVE

APPROXIMATELY THIRTY WOMEN prisoners work the large laundry room at one time while two Serbian guards take turns watching over them. Shayna, Bella, Sarah and Stella all work together in the same washing area. Each is dressed in the same drab camp uniform and performs the same monotonous duties hour after hour, day after day. The laundry load is tremendous and sometimes they work from dawn until dusk. It's now early morning so the day will linger on.

One guard steps forward with a loud announcement, "Attention! Attention!" The women stop their work, look up and listen with a cumulative swallow of apprehension. "We will be visited today by a German SS police officer, head of the Belgrade Military Security Division here in Banjica."

The women's apprehension is now replaced by fear.

"He's in charge of camp security. This is his job, just the building's security, so relax and go back to work." The guard smirks enjoying his power.

The women are momentarily stunned but then begin to whisper among themselves. "Oh, dirty laundry, dirty laundry, and such a wedding present." Shayna attempts to sing.

Bella gives Shayna a hand motion to stop. Shayna notices Bella's signal and slips into a silent depression; she looks away.

"Shayna, have you seen Albert at all?" Stella whispers into her ear.

"No, not even one glimpse. It's like we were never married and I'm still so all alone," Shayna replies in a normal volume. She seems to hold back her anxiety, but her wide eyes give her away.

"Please Shayna," Bella almost begs. "You must try to cope.

Think about the children and what dangers you might cause them with your behavior."

Shayna sighs with a deep grimace and then picks up some men's dirty pants. She goes through the pockets and pulls out two crumpled up pieces of rubber. She holds them up.

"Hey everybody, what are these things?"

Sarah jumps in fast. "Throw those filthy things in the trash can, now!" Shayna flips the rubbers onto the floor. "Yuck! Germs!"

"Now go wash your hands!" Sarah demands. "Men put those rubbers on their privates to screw who knows what, so they don't get a disease."

Shayna turns down her mouth in disgust and scrunches up her hands. "Oh, no!"

"Just go put your hands in the soapy laundry water." Bella motions in forced indifference. She makes yet another attempt to calm down her excitable daughter.

Shayna walks over to the open laundry water and dips her hands. "Now I gotta touch fornicator's dirty rubbers." *I feel sick this time,* Shayna thinks, *I'm so all alone with no husband to talk to. I'm just so miserable that I could die. I hate this place. I hate my life.*

Shayna continues attending school for the remainder of the last month, determined to graduate. Rachel is absent most of the time since the racing incident. She seems unable to ignore the hate and intolerance as well as Shayna does. Although Shayna discounts it most of the time, she is left with a sense of frustration. She can't quite understand or imagine why this is all happening to her. She is angry with herself for tolerating it and not striking back. Deep down she knows the odds are stacked against her and if she retaliates, she will be expelled from school before graduation. They would definitely create some trumped up charges just to get rid of another Jew. Shayna always thought she could control just about anything that life put in her path, but she is becoming more convinced every day that this one is beyond her understanding. *This problem is bigger than I am and beyond me,* Shayna believes. *It's not my fault, but I feel trapped and swept away somewhere in its strangling grip.*

As Shayna sits in the school bleachers at graduation waiting for her confirmation, she hears some boys a few rows back attacking loudly. They are aiming their verbal abuse toward her on purpose. "The Jews killed Christ," one of the male voices yells out. Everyone turns around and looks at him, then frowns at Shayna. They seem to agree with this crazed voice as if it's somehow the very incarnate of God almighty.

Shayna turns her head and yells out to the obnoxious voice behind her. "Jesus Christ was a Jew; the white Romans killed Christ. Read your bible."

A louder male voice blurts out at Shayna in retribution. "You Jews have all the money and we live in poverty so get out of our country."

"It's my country too! Get an education, get a job and then get your own money." Shayna retorts back finally releasing her anger at the voice hiding behind her.

"Screw you, Jew bitch!"

Go to hell, Shayna whispers up under her breath. She keeps her temper in check knowing that these malicious boys want to start a public fight with her intentionally on this graduation day. It's their last chance to bring her down.

"Shayna Weinberg, please come forward for your graduation certificate." The speaker on the front platform calls out as Shayna stands up. She walks slowly and carefully toward the platform, making sure that no one will try to trip her on the way up. Shayna wills herself to continue forward at any cost.

"You haters can't take this away from me," Shayna hears her own voice proclaiming through the clapping hands as she jumps on the stage. She picks up her graduation certificate in sheer determination and triumph.

CHAPTER THIRTEEN

LATER THAT AFTERNOON the SS Security Officer shows up. Two armed German bodyguards enter with him. One stands relaxed at the door with the pleasant observation that all the inmates are women. The other guard follows the officer around. The German officer is about thirty, well-built and extremely handsome. Shayna notices this and decides to be flippant for a moment to relieve her boredom with just a little nonsense. *Maybe I can get an older man like that to just notice me and pay me some fleeting attention.* She weighs the thought in contemplation but neglects to consider any consequences. It's as if she could always be the director of her fate. *Why not? I need just a little fun. This place is so boring and stifling.*

The German security SS officer dresses in a dark police uniform, equally dark boots, a billed hat and wears a swastika armband. His name tag says 'Frolich'. His two Germany army guards dress in dark brownish uniforms, heavy boots, combat hats and also wear swastika arm bands.

Officer Frolich walks around the laundry room and inspects the walls, wired windows and electrical plugs. High tension fills the air. Shayna looks up from her work and intently directs her eyes at him in a schoolgirl enticement, as if he was a teenage boy. Frolich notices her tantalizing self-absorption and walks towards her as he thoroughly enjoys the female eye contact. Shayna immediately lowers her eyes and head, but it's too late. An unfamiliar predator has just been aroused.

Officer Frolich approaches Shayna cautiously. She now stands deathly still, regretting her girlish act of immature teasing. The other women near her appear anxious, even nervous as the intensity spreads. He stops in his tracks as if Shayna has struck his very core.

The Serbian guard interrupts Shayna's frantic-by-now, seduction scene with a reassuring command. "Continue working women, there is nothing to fear," but the sexual tension is much too heavy to stop or even diminish now that it has been set in motion.

Officer Frolich stops behind Shayna with a heavy, hungry awareness. He looks her over and almost touches her body. The women are frozen in fear. He then moves in front of Shayna and touches her chin bringing her face up to his with an extended index finger. Her long hair falls back with its own abandonment as if granting an invitation to fondle.

The German officer gasps in an animal excitement peering into her light brown eyes; their hot glint of terror drives him on. Shayna lowers her head again. Her lips set in a gentle, saintly smile hoping to extinguish his burn with her goodness and sincerity.

Discounting her faint juvenile attempt at control, the German officer stands with Shayna briefly, regaining his composure and then carefully walks away. He glances back over his shoulder at her several times like a stalking tiger. Frolich swaggers a little, measuring her up with his teeth clenched and one eye closed. Shayna's body shakes as she watches him walk towards the door, her eyes wet with dubious tears as a chill of anxiety runs through her spine. His bodyguards exit with him, shutting the door behind them.

CHAPTER FOURTEEN

THE MALE CIVILIAN prisoners line up in rows in the main courtyard. Armed Serbian guards surround them on all sides.

The second ranking Serbian guard pompously paces in front of the crowd. "All able-bodied men will be shipped out tumorrow to the Semlin Sajmiste camp near Belgrade."

The prisoners shudder in fear and anxiety.

"There you will be distributed by trains for various labor assignments."

A loud gasp falls over the trembling crowd.

"Some will be assigned to repair roads, bridges or railroad tracks destroyed by the Allies' bombs. Some will work on farms harvesting crops."

The men whisper sharing their fear and wonder what's to become of them.

"Some will work in the stone quarries; some will log trees for building construction, and some will be shot."

The men are suddenly quiet.

That night Murray, Albert, Henry, Benjamin and Leon all sit together in their barrack's cell talking with a concerned angst. An invisible cloud of sadness fills the air like pollution.

"We have to stay strong or die," Murray holds back. "Or be executed," Henry retorts.

Albert jumps in, "What, dad?"

"Albert, I'm in my sixties, you know that. I will either die from physical exhaustion or be shot as I lay on my tired, worn out back"

A surging panic penetrates Albert and he pushes it back. "Dad, you're a good man and have been a good father to all of us."

"Thank you son, but my time may be coming soon."

"I won't let them shoot you." Albert slumps in a powerless shudder.

"Son, we all must die sometime, and I am getting older."

"I'll..." Albert starts, but Henry cuts him off.

"Thanks, son, but your mother is waiting for me."

Albert glares at Henry startled.

"Yes Albert, I talk to her in my dreams when I'm asleep you know. She's there for me." An eerie silence fills the room and then an accepting release. "Now promise me Albert, that you won't get yourself shot over this."

Albert lingers on Henry in disbelief as though he was lost in a dream and would soon wake up. "I, I don't know, okay, Dad." Albert gets up from his seat on the bed and drags himself away. He lets his mind float out the window into the night sky with sad, desperate eyes. *It's as if I'm trapped in a nether world of violent, surreal cartoon characters.*

Morning arrives with the male prisoners lined up in the main courtyard. Armed guards surround them as usual, and two large open military trucks wait in the distance.

Serbian guard Jingo reads from a paper. "The following men will return to their barracks immediately, no exceptions. The others will get onto the two waiting trucks and again, with no exceptions!"

A loud huff of concerted loathing and then fear follows from the imprisoned crowd of men. Jingo begins reading, "Aleksander Daja, Murray Weinberg, Nikola Novak, Albert Jacobs." Albert's face falls in despondency and then just as quickly turns into a puffed red rage.

Albert turns to Murray. "Where's my Dad? Where did he go?"

Murray looks at Albert in sorrow. "He went to get onto the truck."

"No! No!" Albert shouts out and sprints to the line of men as they wait their turn to get onto the truck. Albert searches frantically for Henry. "Henry Jacobs, Henry Jacobs, where are you? Where are you? Answer me now!"

A voice comes from inside the crowd of men. "I'm here, Albert."

Albert runs toward the voice while pushing men out of the way. They let him through without a fight feeling his pain. Albert runs to his dad and embraces him. Albert's older brother Leon and his brother-in-law Benjamin Zentall stand near Henry.

"You must let me go, Albert. Leon and Benjamin are with me. They will take care of me."

"No! No! I want to go with you. I don't want to stay here!"

Two Serbian guards approach Albert and forcefully grab him. "Go to your barracks immediately!" Jingo demands of Albert.

Henry interrupts, "Albert, think of your sister Sarah and your niece and nephews, think of your wife Shayna."

"No! No! I want to go too. I'll never see you again, Dad."

One Serbian guard throws Albert to the ground and kicks him in the stomach with his heavy boot. His breath leaves his body in a *whoosh* as he doubles over in pain winded, totally helpless and gasping for air. Murray immediately tries to assist him as Albert struggles to his feet coughing, wheezing and finally relenting, physically beaten. Nevertheless, he's still carrying a bitter frown as Murray leads him limping away.

Henry, Leon and Benjamin look back toward Albert and Murray as they climb onto the truck.

That night in the woman's barracks there is no conversation, only weeping. Shayna, Stella and Sarah cry into their blankets as Bella sits in mortified shock, wondering what the future holds.

The same night in the men's barracks, Albert is kneeling in prayer beside his bed. "Blessed are you, Lord, our God, King of the universe, the true judge." A hushed and gloomy Murray watches over him. After his prayer Albert lies down in his bed and squeezes his eyes shut.

CHAPTER FIFTEEN

SHAYNA, STELLA, SARAH and Bella continue working in the laundry room along with the other women. The two-armed guards watch them as usual. Stella lowers her face in tears. "My husband's gone now; I just can't go on."

Sarah steps in, "Stella, you must think of your daughter, Etta. She needs you more than ever now. You are all that she has."

Stella looks up at Sarah and wipes back her tears. "Yes, you're right. I love my daughter."

"My husband's gone too, but hopefully I will see him again after the war," Sarah smiles. Shayna jumps into the conversation. "When is that, Sarah? When is after the war?"

Bella exhales noisily not looking forward to another attempt at controlling the feral Shayna. "Shayna, these people mean business! You must try to manage your emotions."

Shayna then tries to calm down while mumbling to herself, "Okay, Mother, just for you." Bella peers at Shayna and sighs not knowing what to expect next from her willful daughter. The first guard comes forward and shouts an announcement: "Attention all workers! Our German SS police security officer is here again today."

The women drop their laundry work and a startled silence fills the room. Shayna's eyes widen anxiously and her brow furrows. Officer Frolich walks through the door upright and formal, most definitely there for business. His two guards follow him through just as they did previously. One stands at the door entrance and the other follows behind him. Frolich scans the laundry room until he sees Shayna. He then motions to and talks quietly with the two Serbian guards. They both look over at Shayna and then dip their heads in concerted agreement. Officer Frolich then turns and walks out the door with his two guards following behind him.

Shayna stands shaking in dread. What have I done? She reflects to herself. What is this older man going to do to me?

It's the end of the working day in the laundry room and the women line up to leave for the evening. As they go out one by one, the first guard takes Shayna by the arm to stop her from leaving. Shayna freezes. Bella who is in front of Shayna stops briefly and stares back at the guard. The guard motions for Bella to move on and not interfere, but Bella stops outside of the door and glares back in with demanding eyes. The guard glowers in return at Bella who is facing him with a nasty scowl.

"Please let my daughter come with us," Bella begs.

The guard frowns down at Bella. "She will not be harmed. We just want to talk with her."

"About what?" Bella retorts.

"Leave immediately!" The guard orders Bella.

"I want my daughter now!"

The second Serbian guard points a rifle at Bella's head. Bella cautiously pushes the rifle away from her head and leaves. She ambles back toward the women's barracks shrouded in the gloom of a mother's sadness of blind male domination and sexual control.

The two guards that were with Officer Frolich return through the laundry room door, grab Shayna, and attempt to carry her away. Shayna fights and screams as they go. "Put me down! Put me down! I don't want to go!"

CHAPTER SIXTEEN

SHAYNA HAS NOT yet returned to the women's barracks and Bella sits up on her bed worrying, anxious for her return. Walter sits with her and fumbles around with a makeshift toy.

"Where's Shayna?" Walter squints at Bella lost in his toy car world.

"I don't know, Walter darling." Bella holds back the tears as she sinks into a terrified heap. Walter looks up at Bella surprised at his mother's reaction but continues playing with his toy. Bella, Stella and Sarah all sit with their children contemplating the barrack's door and waiting for Shayna to walk through it alive and well.

It is early morning and Bella wakes up startled. She looks for Shayna in the beds, but Shayna is nowhere in sight. Bella walks into the restroom area and calls for Shayna. "Shayna, are you here?" There is no answer, just silence and the rumble of the other women waking up.

Sarah sits up and looks around for Shayna too. Bella is back in the cell and they both sit, waiting for any word or sight of Shayna.

"I wonder where they took her." Sarah speaks softly.

Bella stares at Sarah knowingly, as any mother of a beautiful, young daughter would.

Bella frets nervously as the days pass. "It's been a week now Sarah and still no Shayna."

"I'm so sorry Bella. It looks like Shayna has been kidnapped."

"I have to find Murray and tell him to watch for her."

"Yea, that's a good idea, if you can find him."

Bella gives Sarah a fixed stare of disbelief and then painful acceptance. "I haven't seen Murray since we came here."

Bella closes her eyes and hangs her head. Walter comes over and sits beside his mother, seeming to feel her pain.

CHAPTER SEVENTEEN

ALBERT, MURRAY AND several other male prisoners stand in the main courtyard in front of Jingo and other armed Serbian guards. Jingo holds a clipboard and reads from it. "Albert Jacobs, step forward."

Albert steps forward in a forced attention. "Yes."

"You will now be our camp banker."

Albert squints from under his brow. "What does that mean?"

"You will soon see. New workers are coming into the camp with many suitcases and you will be responsible for the transfer of their money."

"What?" Albert guffaws. "You want me to steal innocent people's money for you?" Jingo twists up his face. "Do you want the job, or do you want a bullet?"

Albert stares at Jingo stone faced and reflects silently. *You ugly piece of trash; you're the lowest scum of the earth.*

Jingo continues, "You have two choices, my friend Albert. I have guards here who will be more than happy to pull the trigger right now!"

Albert stands back in frustration and silently thinks. *Why do I have to deal with this human garbage?*

"Well, Mr. Albert, what will it be? Make up your mind, now!"

Albert looks over to Murray who is nodding his head up and down. "Okay, guards, ready your rifles," Jingo orders.

Albert flinches as he is motioned to move away from the other men so he can be shot. *Maybe I should just let them shoot me and get it over with.* Albert imagines himself dead on the ground and no one really cares. *They will just haul my body away and incinerate it.*

"Okay Albert," Jingo orders. "Move away from the others now! A bullet is waiting for you." Albert refuses to move. Two Serbian guards move towards Albert. They grab him by the arms and try to pull him away from the other men as Albert fights back relentlessly.

"Albert!" Murray yells at him. "What good are you if you're dead?"

Albert weighs the bad against the worst, *I feel so small and so outnumbered.* Suddenly as if divinity has finally peaked through, Albert stares at Murray. "Ah, okay then, but against my will, I'll take the job. God forgive me," Albert relents.

Jingo and his pack of Serbian baying hounds break out in loud barks of laughter at Albert as they release him.

Albert glares at Jingo in revulsion. *I wish I could vomit.*

With his tightly drawn mouth and dark penetrating eyes, Jingo ignores it and continues on. It's as if he was raised on insults and nonverbal intimidations his entire life, "Murray Weinberg, next."

Murray steps forward at a forced attention. "Yes."

"You will be in charge of all the electricity in the camp, all the security fences, the circuitry, all the lights, the plugs etc." Jingo smiles haughtily seeming to relish his own importance.

"Yes." Murray reluctantly mumbles and stands back.

Albert lowers his head in dejection and misery. *I will pay all of you rotting carcasses back.*

CHAPTER EIGHTEEN

WITH THE CLOUDS breaking just at sunrise and the air crisp and brittle, Albert stands and talks with a Slavic woman in the main courtyard.

"What? Bella knows it?" Albert questions the female inmate.

"Yes." The Slavic woman asserts. "I saw two German guards carry Shayna into barracks number ten. She was shrieking and trying desperately to break free from them."

"What?" Albert is stunned. "Are you sure it was number ten and Shayna?"

"Positive." The woman shakes her head affirmatively.

"Thanks!" Albert waves at her and without another word turns and runs head long in a flustered rush to barracks ten.

No one is in sight as Albert swings open the surprisingly unlocked main door of barracks ten. Once inside Albert secretly slithers up to three different offices. He tries each doorknob, but they are all locked and temporarily vacant of workers. As Albert looks up, he sees the signs over each door. The first door is labeled: COMMANDANT WILLY FRIEDRICH. The sign over the second door is labeled: CAMP ADMINISTRATOR, SVETOZAR VUJKOVIC and the third door is labeled: CAMP BANKER. *Oh my God*, Albert muses to himself. *This is my office, I'm the camp banker.*

Albert shakes it off in angst and continues with his exploration. There is a cough in the large restroom and Albert goes to investigate. He peeks around the corner of the open door. A pompous looking, older Serbian man brushes his teeth and spits in the sink. A toilet flushes.

Albert leaves the restroom area and quietly searches through the entirety of barracks number ten. There is no sign of Shayna anywhere. Albert leaves and shuts the main door behind him thinking, *I hope I never have to meet that arrogant lowlife I saw brushing his rotten teeth.*

Murray and Albert sit together in their barrack's bedroom cell.

"Today a Slavic woman told me that Shayna was kidnapped," Albert reports. Murray is speechless with a gapped mouth.

"Yes," Albert rants. "The woman works with my sister Sarah and Bella in the laundry room."

"What?" Murray gasps in horror.

"Bella knows about it and she's trying to find Shayna. The Slavic woman says that Bella believes Shayna is still alive somewhere here in Banjica."

Murray clamps his fists together in rage and irritation. "So now, they steal our children."

"Yeah, and now the Germans and their illiterate goons steal my wife." Albert falls back onto his bed thinking, *talking about it makes me even angrier.*

Murray holds back his wrath, still clenching his fists together waiting for the right moment and caught in a silent scream.

CHAPTER NINETEEN

THE SIGN ABOVE the camp banker's office in barracks ten spells out Albert Jacob's name, much to his chagrin. Albert reluctantly sits at a large desk towards the back of the room. There are two German armed guards and two Belgrade special police officers with him.

The commanding Belgrade police officer, who stands unusually short, hands Albert a large accounting book. "You will keep track of everything coming and going out of Banjica."

"And what is that?" Albert questions.

"All Jews were previously told to register their real estate with the Belgrade Administration Headquarters of Jewish Property. We have records."

"Thieves."

"Watch your mouth!"

Albert looks away to avoid more trouble but grits his teeth in a closed tight aversion.

"You will check our records and transfer all real estate to one of our many upstanding State mortgage banks right here on our lists." The Belgrade officer points at a paper. "Every day you will ready a deposit of money transfers, precious metals, precious stones and personal items to the German National Bank."

"Personal items?" Albert tilts his head. "Banks don't take personal items."

"This bank does."

"How?" Albert squints in anticipation.

"A concealed account will help launder valuables given to us from the nice Jews like fine art or some smelly old antique candelabra."

"What?" Albert drains out a piece of himself in thought, *menorah candelabra, you disrespectful piece of human trash.* "You force me to sin against my God," Albert blurts out.

The German army guards treat Albert to rolling laughter, but the Belgrade officer breaks the amusement. "Gentlemen! Gentleman! This is why our good friend Albert was chosen for this banking job."

"How's that?" Albert demands in a harsh growl almost ready to bite.

"Albert, you better not steal one cent from the nice Germans or bang! Bang!"

Albert is enraged. "I wouldn't steal one cent of your blood money against my people, or any of the other people that you murder!"

"Exactly, Albert, welcome to the German National Bank. May I help you, sir?" The Belgrade officer gloats in his own authority as his fellow guards roll in laughter.

Albert stares in not just resentment but loathing at the little man before him. *You're smaller than you appear to be.* Albert gets in the last laugh but to himself. *If I had a gun right now all of you scum would be dead.*

To this very day when facing a challenging situation, Wilhelm Frolich always seems to return to the memories of his seventh-grade swim class. *It's said that early childhood traumas shape your adult mentality,* Wilhelm considers. *I've tried to push my middle school years out of my memory, but they keep coming back to haunt me.*

Wilhelm loves to swim and just float in the water. It mysteriously pulls him into a primeval state of mind making him feel a contented connection to the entire universe. *I can see with my heart and feel love for the sky, trees and all of God's animals,* he thinks out loud. He dreamily focuses his undivided attention on his mind's eye. Visiting the local zoo and communicating with the animals is extremely enjoyable to him. He's especially fond of the sea lions and sea turtles. He imagines himself drifting away into their sublime watery world, engulfed in the timelessness and beauty of

Mother Nature.

This day is very special for him because he has just turned twelve years old and it's his birthday. His mother and father would be waiting for him at home after school with cake. They would also have surprise presents like that new bicycle that would give him his newfound freedom. He had dreamed of riding through the neighborhood instead of walking and putting up with the bullies who confront him on foot. With the bicycle, he could just fly away like a bird and leave them in his wind. Good luck chasing him because he knows every nook and cranny hiding place in the forest.

Wilhelm has a few friends his own age that he plays with in the nearby German forest, but mostly he is a loner and stays to himself. On occasion he plays checkers with his neighbor Bruno, a boy his age who is confined to a wheelchair because of crippled legs. They both are now learning to play chess with the help of Wilhelm's father. Mr. Frolich spends almost every weekend setting up chess matches for the two boys, or any other neighbor boy or girl that wants to participate.

Several boys and girls came a few times at first, but then lost interest despite Mr. Frolich's cookies, fruity drink treats and toy prizes for the winners. Wilhelm and Bruno eventually are the only two remaining chess match challengers.

Wilhelm glides through the water this special day in his German military school's swimming pool. He's thinking about skipping lunch after the swim class is over and enjoying his birthday floating alone. He would go into the locker room and change into his regular school uniform when he hears the ten-minute warning bell. That would give him plenty of time to get to his next class. The swim coach left for lunch and no students, including Wilhelm, are allowed to be in the pool without supervision. Wilhelm had hidden underwater when the coach checked the pool before leaving for lunch. Wilhelm smirks to himself with the sneaky dodge of tricking him.

After a few minutes of peaceful water soaring, Wilhelm hears vague echoes of whispers bouncing off the tiles in the locker room. Knowing the bullies in his class, he imagines what is coming next and braces himself, hiding along the edge of the pool so as not to be seen. But somehow these rogue boys got wind of Wilhelm tricking the swim coach. They remained in the locker room by standing up on the toilets and quietly hiding after class to confront Wilhelm who is in the pool by himself.

Suddenly the boys, who are only a few years older, appear along the edges of the pool near where Wilhelm is hiding. He recognizes the tallest from a summer baseball camp that he had dropped out of due to bullies. The two shorter boys had also been at the same camp and all were German, just like him. As this gang of three approaches the side of the swimming pool near Wilhelm, the taller boy, who appears to be the leader, speaks first.

"There's the little sissy that can't bat or catch a ball," he points to Wilhelm scowling as if he is entitled to pass judgment. The other two boys edge themselves closer to Wilhelm and try to grab him out of the water.

"I hear you're a little momma's boy that plays chess." The tall boy spits out in revulsion while encouraging the other two boys to be more forceful in grasping Wilhelm. "Just a little pussy... ha, ha."

Yelling from the water Wilhelm gawks up at the tall boy as he instinctively paddles out into the middle of the pool. "Leave me alone! You're not my boss! You couldn't boss me around at camp and you can't boss me now!"

"Go in after him!" The tall boy screams ordering the other two boys to give chase. "What? I'm not getting wet," the first boy refuses the orders.

"Yes, you are!" The tall boy screams at him. "Both of you girls get in now or I'll pick you up and throw you in!"

"No!" The first boy screams back to the tall boy as he turns around and walks away.

"Coward!" The tall boy shouts after him as he goes. "Go for it!" The tall boy orders the remaining boy who looks at the tall boy and then at the water and cringes.

The shorter boy shakes his head no. The tall boy goes over and kicks the short boy's legs out from under him and throws him into the pool. The boy squeals with reluctance hitting the water with a wild splatter as his arms and legs thrash in resistance. Gasping for breath, he submerges, gradually recovering his evil self and glances around to see that Wilhelm is climbing up the ladder and out of the pool at the deep end.

"Get him now!" The tall boy screeches as he runs toward Wilhelm who is out of the pool and running toward the locker room. The tall boy chases Wilhelm who is barefoot and grabs him by the arm spinning him around as Wilhelm slips to the wet tile floor. The tall boy then kicks Wilhelm in the stomach with his military boot. Wilhelm doubles over grabbing his stomach and winces in a deep gasp for air. The tall boy then drags Wilhelm feet first back to the edge of the pool and using his boot kicks him into the water again. Wilhelm drops into the pool like lead with a sinking splash. In the water, the other boy is on Wilhelm in an instant. Wilhelm, still struggling for air, is being ducked under and held. His bubbles rise to the surface and his hands lift into the air above as if trying to grab onto anything. The tall boy gives out a sharp, loud snort as if he has won a perverted war, but unexpectedly Wilhelm breaks free by kicking the shorter boy in the groin. The boy bends over into the water grabbing his crotch and letting out a deafening scream as he submerges.

Wilhelm swims back toward the deep end and climbs back up the ladder. The tall boy is waiting and kicks him back down into the water. The other boy, having somewhat recovered, has somehow found the strength to jump on Wilhelm again. Both boys are matched in height, weight and strength as they tumble and fight in the water.

In a last chance survival rush of adrenaline, Wilhelm doubles up his fist and punches the other boy square in the face causing the boy to sink in the water. Suddenly Wilhelm sees the swim coach diving into the pool to rescue the boy. It only takes seconds for the coach to pull the boy up and drag him out of the pool. The boy's broken nose is bleeding profusely and scarlet fills the surface of the pool. While the swim coach gives the second boy resuscitation, Wilhelm drags himself up the ladder and out of the pool.

The swim coach bellows like a foghorn at Wilhelm. "Go to the office... now... and tell them to call an ambulance!"

With a deep-set frown covering his twisted face, Wilhelm glares down on the swim coach for a short pause wanting to yell out his reasons for not going for help. *Those bastards tried to kill me... and then just disappear as if I accidentally drown alone in the pool*, he rationalizes to himself. The coach shouts out again, this time in anger at Wilhelm.

Still in deep shock Wilhelm considers shouting his reasoning back in anger, but then slowly nods his head in the affirmative to the swim coach. As Wilhelm limps away almost crawling back into the locker room, he scours the area for the other two accomplices, but they have conveniently disappeared, leaving their mess behind them just like in a horror show.

CHAPTER TWENTY

TWO WEEKS PASS and Shayna is still missing. Her family's search for her continues in confidence as no one else in Banjica really cares if she is missing. A seven-foot high chain-link fence separates a back house from the prisoner's barracks. Many inmates aren't even aware that the house exists. A perpetually locked gate in the middle of the fence provides the only walk-in access to the house, not only shutting it off physically, but secrets must dwell there.

Furnishings inside the house are sufficient and necessary without being gaudy. Shayna sits on a sofa in the middle of it all. She wears a fine dress; new shoes and her hair falls about her shoulders. An older Jewish woman serves her tea and pastries.

"Thank you, Mimi." Shayna smiles ever so politely at Mimi not really knowing yet if she likes it here or not in this strange but comfortably familiar world.

"Will that be all, Misses?"

"Yes, Ma'am, I guess so."

The German SS security officer, Frolich, from the laundry barracks walks into the room. He is tall, handsome and physically attractive just as Shayna first noticed him in her youthful game of chance. "So how did you sleep last night, love?" He inquires as Shayna just sighs and falls back onto the sofa a bit nervous and anxious. No answer, so he persists, "Shayna, are you alright this morning?"

"Well, the truth is I'm concerned about my family. They'll be wondering where I am."

"I guess I knew that all along."

"They are my family, you know."

"I know who your father is, and he has been made head of the camp's electrical security, far from being in danger."

"So you say."

"And your mother, I know who she is too, and your little brother, Walter is it?" Shayna looks at him in surprise. Officer Frolich smiles at her.

"I'm worried about them. My Jewish family is in danger."

"I thought that we agreed not to bring that up or talk about it, at all, Shayna. It's very dangerous."

"Yes, I know, but," she almost whimpers cutting herself off.

"You know that it's against the law for us to be together."

"So, you will get into trouble?"

"Hardly," Officer Frolich shrugs, "maybe a slap in the face or a hard kick in the ass."

"Is that all?" Shayna's brow falls in skepticism and then grievance.

"The Commandant turns his head on discrete sex, but I can only marry a German woman." Shayna narrows her eyes in immediate agitation.

"Most of the other officers and guards either have a secret mistress too or visit the Gestapo run brothels."

"What? There are brothels in the camps?"

"Yes, men need women and sex to function normally. It's a stress release." Officer Frolich squints holding his forehead as his eyes close silently floating somewhere in his memory. *The first time that I was taken to a brothel in a large camp, I was scared shitless. It was a sad ruthless place guarded by round the clock security. Both Serbian and German guards were waiting in line to enter the brothel with money in hand. Dim red lights and smoke came from the twenty something rooms full of pitiful women who I was told are often shot after they get sick or are no longer useful.* Officer Frolich weaves and falls back into his seat in a full frown, not at all happy with his recollections.

Shayna blurts out to Frolich, "Are you alright, Frolich? Where are you?"

Officer Frolich shakes out of his fleeting daze. "Ah, yeah, I guess so, and those guards can thank Heinrich Himmler for his brothel master plan."

"What?" Shayna stares wondering where that came from.

Officer Frolich reflects again going back into his recall. A brawl broke out that night at the brothel between two Serbian guards in the waiting line. They were punching and fighting each other over what, I don't know, but the security guards broke it up immediately. Then I heard a woman's loud scream coming from one of the brothel rooms, and then a loud gunshot, and then a woman's frantic crying. Frolich shifts into a limp slump on his chair.

"Okay now," Shayna shakes Officer Frolich. "You were drifting off again."

"What did you say? What? I would never go into those horrible brothels again. They're pure hell."

Shayna gives him a hard look. "So, this defilement of blood mixing is for German women to follow and not German men?"

Officer Frolich mumbles to himself in reluctant agreement.

"Isn't there a patch that the... ah sinners wear?"

"Yes, Aryan women and Jewish men who are racial defilers wear a visible colored patch, both black and yellow triangles but inverted differently."

"And, what patch do the Aryan men wear for their racial defilement?"

"There are no patches for Aryan men. I suppose that disgusts you?"

"Yes, it does!" Shayna's voice holds a nervous edge as she enters new territory. "What about diseases?"

"The women in the brothels are checked once a week by doctors. All are overseen of course by the illustrious Heinrich Himmler, the Godfather of all procurers."

"This whole thing is really sick."

"Sick yes, but rape has always been a weapon of war. It's a military strategy."

"What? How is that?"

"Well to start off, rape destroys local populations, relationships, marriages. It destroys cultures and religious traditions."

"Oh, that makes it alright to do this to women and their outcast, abandoned babies?"

"Well, I suppose not."

"Then why are you here, doing this?"

"You see, Shayna, I was conscripted. You know, drafted into the German army." Shayna nods at him catching a glimpse of sadness.

"Not every German citizen agrees with Hitler."

A thoughtful look fills her face.

"Peaceful Germans can be shot as war resisters."

Shayna's surprise turns into a hard-facial expression as she looks away.

"My father is one of them. He's a retired law professor and the Regime made him a diplomat at the German Embassy against his will."

"So, does he kill Jews?" Shayna asks as a matter of fact.

"No actually, he was being investigated for being too lenient with Jews when he had a mild heart attack from all the stress."

Shayna gives him a curious glance, wondering about such a decent German.

"He and my mother just try to avoid the war. What else can they do?"

Shayna winces in thought.

"I have a degree in electrical engineering, but I really just want to live my life in peace."

Shayna asks sarcastically, "So, you are a prisoner too?"

"Well, something like that."

Shayna lets out a loud sigh of confusion.

"I don't get involved in killing people. I just check the electrical fences and other securities in the camp. It is just like the job that I gave to your father."

Shayna glances away briefly. She has had enough of war talk and changes the subject. "Do you use those rubbers every time that we have sex?"

"Yes, I do."

"What if I get pregnant anyway?"

"Well, it depends on what happens."

Shayna turns away from him as if dealing with a deep anger. Helplessness soon catches hold and visibly falls over her, making her feel like a caged canary.

"Oh come on, Shayna," he cajoles. "Our attraction is so intense. I haven't been this excited for years."

"Oh, so this is only about you?"

Officer Frolich is speechless and looks away as he has been exposed.

"And where does that leave me?" Shayna looks at him inquisitively.

Officer Frolich readjusts himself in the chair. "I don't really know, Shayna, I'm only thirty years old and that leaves me still ignorant and stupid."

Shayna becomes cold and distant.

Officer Frolich is briefly silent trying to reestablish his footing. "I guess we should just carry on as nature would have us. Shayna, I don't know what else to say. I suppose I'm just a dunce."

Shayna gives him a fixed glare.

"And for me love, nature's starting again, right now."

"I'm a married woman." She demands.

"You were a virgin."

Shayna scowls in anger.

"I'm really sorry if I hurt you."

Shayna closes her eyes as if to disappear.

"Don't dream too long, love. I'm getting hungry again and you taste so sweet. Nature is knocking on our door again. Come on love, let's answer it."

Shayna passes him a dirty look.

"Shayna... it's the birds and the bees," he smiles trying to make her laugh.

Without laughing Shayna falls back into the sofa. Wilhelm moves in towards her with lust in his eyes.

CHAPTER TWENTY-ONE

FOUR OPEN MILITARY trucks pull into Banjica Concentration Camp. Approximately two hundred people of mixed ethnicities exit. There are men, women and children carrying suitcases and bags. Sixteen multi-ethnic Yugoslav partisan rebels also get off the truck.

All the new prisoners stand in the main courtyard. It's a cold day and they're wrapped in their dirty coats. Some limp and lean on each other as they move away from the trucks. Five Serbian guards approach them.

The first Serbian guard commands, "Men to the right, women to the left."

Everyone moves in frozen anxiety and worry like they have just landed on an alien planet. Albert and Murray watch from the side as the prisoners settle in and wait for their next instructions.

The Serbian guard continues, "All people deposit your luggage and bags in a pile to your left side including all jewelry that you are wearing. It will all be returned to you later." Most prisoners are worn out and starving. They begin to drop their bags onto the community pile and return to where they had previously been waiting.

There are about fifty Gypsy men, women and children standing with a definite no planted on their faces. They are clearly refusing to relinquish their bags.

Jingo notices this indiscretion and stomps forward like a petty dictator. His voice screams with a ragged threatening edge at the assembly. The Gypsies gape at him with stubbornness as the irritation increases the deep line between Jingo's brows. Then an abrupt personality change washes over him as resignation falls across his face. He will deal with them later because it appears that he has bigger tasks ahead. *These Gypsies will not test the mighty Jingo in public.*

"Women and children will go into women's barracks number two. Civilian men will go into men's barracks number three." The first Serbian guard points toward the barracks.

The Gypsies mumble and talk among themselves. One older Gypsy man speaks up. "We Gypsies want to stay together."

The second Serbian guard yells imposingly at him. "Silence or you will be executed!"

The Gypsy speaks out regardless. "You're going to shoot us anyway, so what's the difference?"

The second Serbian guard goes over to the older Gypsy man and threatens him with his rifle. The Gypsy says nothing.

The first Serbian guard gives more orders. "The partisans will go to barracks number four and all Gypsies, men, women and children will go to barracks number five."

Albert and Murray walk away toward their barracks. "Why do they separate the Gypsies, Murray?"

"They have a totally different culture from most ethnic Slavs, Serbs or Jews."

Albert takes it in.

"Most Jewish people are manageable, but the Gypsies have no regard for the Germans or the Serbian guards at all."

"Why should they?"

"They shouldn't, Albert, but it causes a lot of trouble."

"So, the Gypsies will riot?"

"Maybe. You see, Jews are taught to negotiate and compromise. The Gypsies just lash out at the Germans."

"So, what will the Germans do?" Albert looks quizzical.

"Eventually, just shoot them on the spot!"

Albert winces.

"Most Gypsies refuse to work in the German labor camps. This makes them worthless to the Regime."

Albert flinches, worried and abruptly stops walking. "Murray, why are we here? Did we die and go to Purgatory?"

"I don't know Albert; I really don't know."

The newcomers into Banjica are adrift, worn out and unsure of their next move. Life in the camp has its way with them and yet they are still alive, living and trying to get from one day to the next despite the enormous life challenges they know awaits them.

Albert sits at his bank desk in barracks ten and launders money. Two Serbian State guards and two German army guards take turns watching him.

The new prisoner's luggage is temporarily stored in a large pile in a back-storage bin of barracks number ten. Jingo and the Serbian administrator of Banjica, Svetozar Vujkovic, stand in the storage bin. They are going through the newly arrived suitcases and duffle bags before they are officially opened by the Germans. Vujkovic is a man intoxicated by his own power. He was a pre-war Serbian policeman who now enthusiastically collaborates with the Germans.

Jingo pulls out some women's clothes from a large suitcase and tosses them aside. "Can't wear a dress," he shrinks but reconsiders picking up the dress again and examines it closer.

Vujkovic chuckles at Jingo. "At least not in public," he laughs as he opens the next suitcase and pulls out the contents. A rich man's custom made black three-piece suit and a pair of hand made two toned black and white leather shoes fall to the floor. Jingo stares at them for a fast second and then bends down to grab them up for himself.

"Oh no you don't, you filthy thief." Vujkovic grumbles at Jingo, ramming him away with brute force. Jingo falls back, catching himself on a large box.

"I want both of those for myself." Jingo comes back with a swipe at Vujkovic.

Vujkovic, a menacing man with a tight frown and raised eyebrows, grabs up both the custom suit and shoes. He clings to them as if clutching his future.

"You bastard, you can't have them both; give me either the suit or the shoes."

"Screw you Jingo, they're both mine, I found them."

Jingo grabs the two-tone shoes away from Vujkovic and shoves him to the floor with the other hand. Vujkovic still grips the suit, "You low life scum, get your own shoes."

Jingo shoots Vujkovic a dart of a glare holding the shoes tight, a mask of grim resolution crosses his face. "These shoes are mine you bastard, keep the goddamn Jew suit."

What a surprise when Wilhelm Frolich opens his mailbox and finds a letter addressed to him from his high school. Eager to see the contents, he rips open the envelope and glares at the letter-head. It's from the soccer coach personally inviting him to try out for the soccer team.

He chuckles to himself as he stumbles with his long, gangly legs into the house. He places the letter on the dresser in his room. He might give it some thought later, but for what reason he has no idea.

Reluctant and mostly uninterested in sports, Wilhelm decides to save face and just show up. He will be ready but won't give it much effort. The only reason seems to be social acceptability and to show some high school spirit. He has a bookworm reputation as a chess playing loner and this could be an opportunity to change that. Dressed in his gym pants and shoes, Wilhelm stands on the soccer field and looks around at his fellow students. Two of the top school male athletes share the field with him and he watches as they primp and preen, flexing their muscles in their bravado. For a moment he considers himself prancing around like a rooster too, shaking his feathers and wooing the cheerleaders, but that thought soon fades away. He wonders just why he is forcing himself to be here when he obvious has no interest in participating in throwing or kicking any kind of balls around, except maybe the kind that bully him.

When the soccer coach motions for him to come forward and be tested, Wilhelm freezes in his tracks. He seems to be mentally beating himself up because he has actually shown up to make a fool out of himself again at the public athletic tryouts.

I need to study my chemistry and math and not be out here trying to be a tough guy. Wilhelm pushes the words out of his head. I need to be an engineer, not a sports politico. Why can't I just get that through my thick skull and accept myself the way I am?

The soccer coach blows his whistle for Wilhelm to come forward and show why he should be included in their brash ranks. Whatever Wilhelm thought he previously had to prove, wasn't enough to force any action from him, or move him forward. *Why did I come here?* Wilhelm folds his body into himself as he crosses his arms over his chest in a protective gesture and ignores the coach.

"Out of my way, you silly little girl," the team captain screams at Wilhelm, threatening to push him to the ground if he doesn't move.

The soccer coach blows his whistle at the captain, giving Wilhelm another chance to resurrect his courage and give the tryout another shot, but Wilhelm continues to stand dead in his tracks like a stalled car that you just can't push. The coach finally relents with no further comments and moves on to the next potential recruit. When the coach's back is turned, the team captain encourages the other soccer players with silent hand signals to push Wilhelm off the track.

One of the other ball players pulls in behind Wilhelm, silently whispering to him in a low growling, sexually tinged voice. "I see you a lot with that crippled boy in the wheelchair... you pounding him in the ass or something?"

Wilhelm's face falls, but he represses his anger and tries to step out of the way. The whispering ball player's harassment continues. "We never see you with any girls... you a queer?"

Wilhelm looks away disgusted, then to the soccer coach for help, but to no avail. At the moment the coach is engaged in an intense conversation with the team captain. Tension begins to pull at Wilhelm's posture and tighten his neck tendons as a touch of sickness fills his gut. The same ball player persists by again whispering into Wilhelm ear. This time he uses a heavy breath of lusty desire. "Or is it you who wants it in the ass?"

"That's enough!" Wilhelm drops his arms along with any other defenses that he has saved up. His fingers thrust together like knotted tree roots as he turns to meet the whispering boy. The boy just stands there wearing a dumb smile mixed with a sense of superiority and a smirk of childish ego. Wilhelm ponders breaking the whisperer's jaw but then stops, relinquishing any resistance.

Why waste my fist on this imbecile? My father always says, 'Anyone who angers you conquers you.' Wilhelm swirls and stomps off the soccer field in total repulsion. Team laughter follows him as he goes.

CHAPTER TWENTY-TWO

SHAYNA AND WILHELM sit in the living room, drinking tea and eating cake. Shayna is wearing a relaxed heavy winter dress and a warm vest over it. "I'm thinking about leaving," she blurts out softly but firmly to Officer Frolich. She wipes a spot of frosting from her mouth.

Frolich stares intently at her. "You'll miss the cake."

Shayna ignores the joke. "What if I escape in the middle of the night and go back to my husband Albert?"

"What?" Frolich pinches up his face. His worry is justified, and then he helplessly relents. "Oh, go ahead Shayna. You're not a prisoner here. I'll miss you a lot, but you can leave anytime that you want."

Shayna jumps to her feet. "Then I'm leaving right now. I'm going back to the barracks." Shayna gets up, takes her army coat out of the closet and puts it on. She wraps a heavy bland scarf around her neck anticipating the deep cold and looks away with mixed emotions. She appears to want to stay in safety and security, but with equal desperation wants to go. Frolich falls into a frozen body as Shayna prepares to leave. When she turns around, anguished eyes peer back at him with uncertainty, but then just as quickly disappear again into assurance.

Officer Frolich silently watches her go out the door, unable to control the feral, young girl and not really wanting to try. *If she loves me fine, but if she doesn't then I must face it,* Frolich concedes to himself in silence. *That's what I get for messing around with kids.*

Shayna marches up to the locked gate that guards the house. Mimi unlocks the gate for her and Shayna strides through the chain-link fence, back up to the camp as the freezing air bites her face.

It's early evening in the Gypsy barracks. Women and children prepare to sleep in separate cells apart from the men who sleep in their own small cell. There is no heat in either area, so the women and children huddle together for warmth as blankets are scarce. If it is an especially cold night, a husband may sneak into the women's cell to keep his wife and children warm, but sex and partying is never encouraged among the captives.

Shayna walks into women's barracks two towards Bella's cell. A strong stench hits her in the face like a thrown pie. Shayna stops short and inhales the air inside the barracks as her eyes fill with water and she coughs. She wrinkles up her nose in disgust and hears a whiny squeak coming from her throat. She wonders where it came from.

Shayna sees Bella and runs towards her. Bella drops everything and opens her arms wide as Shayna falls into them. Tears fill both of their eyes as Walter chokes back his tears while giving Shayna a big sloppy hug. Shayna picks Walter up off the ground as he fights to be put down.

"Where you been Shayna?" Walter demands. "Mom's been so upset all the time."

"Shayna," Bella whimpers, "We thought that you were dead."

Shayna rolls up into herself. "I'm sorry Mom, but here I am, still alive."

"How could you do this to your poor, old Mother? I could have died of sorrow over this."

"Oh, Mom," Shayna sighs, not really grasping the severity of her mother's despondency. "I'm so sorry, but I was kidnapped and taken away. It's not my fault."

Bella falls quiet.

Walter breaks the momentary silence with a loud sneeze, blows his nose and tumbles onto his bed curling up under a cover for warmth. Bella sits down beside him and gently caresses him for heat retention.

"Still no heat in here?" Shayna shivers with the cold falling over her. She doesn't know what emotion to feel or how to react yet to her new situation.

"Girlie, you still have a lot to learn." Bella looks up at her and holds Walter even closer.

With the addition of another hundred women and children, the women's barracks is overcrowded and overflowing with stress. Thirty women now inhabit Bella's two-family cell. There is fierce competition for the few worn out mattresses and smelly old blankets available. Most of the women and children sleep on the cell's floor in newly scattered straw. They are huddled up with each other for warmth during the intense subzero winter nights, sleeping like cattle and being treated not much better.

Several Serbian guards appear at the barracks door. Jingo blathers to the spilled-over crowds of hungry women. "Our food rations have been cut in half. Sorry but we have to cut back."

The embittered crowd starts to mumble and whine with the ache of an empty stomach.

"If there are fights or arguments, the perpetrators will face the firing squad!" Jingo suddenly changes personalities and yells like a madman.

Everyone suddenly becomes deathly quiet as fear takes over. Several of the other Serbian guards bring in baskets of dried bread, potato peels and hard corn.

"You'll have to find a way to mash all of this up... up... up." Jingo laughs out of his head as though he's been drinking and flaunts his new two toned black and white leather shoes.

Shayna stands up and screams back at Jingo. "You can't do this! We are human beings!" Jingo notices who Shayna is and lowers his grimacing face at her into a demon's mask as if the devil will remember. The other guards laugh at the bold Shayna. She considers Jingo's silent threat no more than a mild slap in the face. *You're a monster,* she contemplates with a defiant stare.

Jingo spits on the barrack floor in a repulsive delight that's not about anything more than his own distorted amusement. Then Jingo and his goons leave, still chuckling as more than a whiff of alcohol permeates the air.

About thirty adult Gypsies gather to talk in the main area of their barracks. They eat dried up bread, raw cabbage and drink water from a makeshift table. No smiles or camaraderie are present, but they do the best with what they have for the moment.

CHAPTER TWENTY-THREE

SHAYNA SAUNTERS INTO the main courtyard of the camp, hoping for some sun and to stay warm for a while. The wind rips her dress and vest nearly off. Her army coat and scarf is gone, along with her wedding ring, lifted by a chilly barracks thief with a taste for gold. Her long dark brown hair tosses about in the wind like the chaos and disruption that is everywhere. "Where can I find food?" Thinking out loud to herself, she searches around for a plan in the morning air. *There must be an answer somewhere; I just have to find it.*

Suddenly Shayna spots Albert in the distance as he walks aimlessly toward barracks ten and his miserable job. She runs after him with the swiftness of an antelope being chased by a cheetah following the growling in its empty stomach.

"Albert, Albert!" She yells. The wind snatches the words out of her mouth and carries them back to her. She falters briefly, but then her hunger drives her on.

"Albert, Albert!" She tries again even louder waving her hands in the air like an umpire screaming for a foul, without considering who might be in ear shot or watching her.

Albert turns around in stark surprise, his mouth drops open as he abandons all of his previous thoughts and runs toward Shayna. They fall into a long desperate hug and Albert kisses her as if the world wasn't even noticing.

"Oh, Shayna, I've looked everywhere for you. Where have you been?"

Shayna starts to tear. She stares glassy eyed at him seeming to hold in a secret as the wind blows against her face and freezes the tears.

"Tell me, tell me! Where have you been? I love you."

"Oh Albert, is this really you? I can hardly believe my eyes."

"Yes. Don't ever leave me again. Please, my life is so lonely without you Shayna." He says her name as if pleading.

Shayna examines him up close in the morning sun. He looks older and more rugged now and has frown lines between his eyes, and I know why.

A glimmer of hope springs into Albert's dark brown eyes and he gives her his most joyful smile. Perhaps remembering happier days together, like walking in the woods and holding hands, from another time and another place.

It is night again and Shayna attempts to sleep in Bella's small bed with her mother and Walter. There is no room for her, and she falls to the floor. Shayna twists up with only her soiled dress and vest on as she rolls around in the matted straw. She tries to cover herself with the straw as she shivers and shakes from the freezing cold. The wind blows in through the holes in a broken window stuffed with random pieces of paper. Shayna digs deep into the straw and covers her face with it making an effort to get some sleep.

The next morning Shayna wakes up to the sound of footsteps around her in the barracks. Someone has urinated on the floor near her and her dress and vest is wet with the stench of it. Shayna jumps to her feet with the urine dripping from her clothing.

Bella and Walter are awake and sit on their bed across from three strange Slavic women. They pass Shayna curious glances as if she is an unwelcome intruder. *Which one of you nasty old women pissed on me?* Shayna reflects in her head. *This place is a human zoo.*

Bella glances at the urine dripping from Shayna and sighs as if this were just another boring common, exasperating event. "There's a water bucket in the sink, dip the cold water out with a cup onto your clothes. Please don't get any urine in it because we use it for drinking too."

"Okay Mother, but when do we get more food?" Shayna looks at Bella, waiting for the answer as if she's a schoolgirl again.

The three Slavic women laugh at Shayna like she's their radio show.

"The food's all gone." Bella states with indifference, not wanting to feel too devastated. Shayna's eyes fall in despair. Bella and Walter snuggle together in desperate, quiet sadness.

CHAPTER TWENTY-FOUR

SHAYNA WAITS BY the front door entrance of barracks ten. It is early morning and Albert walks to work as usual. "Shayna, I'm so happy to see you."

Shayna pulls her urine stained clothes tight against her body, a note of weariness and irritation creeps into her voice. "Do you have anything that you can give me to eat?" She appears awkward and fumbles in her pockets. Not finding anything she crosses her arms behind her back in a calculated repose.

Albert is silent for a moment, studies her and then gives a nod. "Yea, sure."

"Can you give me some extra for my mother and brother too?"

"I can give you my food for the day."

"No, can't you get some extra food since you're the banker?" Shayna finds herself easing back a little away from him in case he says that he can't do it.

"I'll try. Come back at noon. They put the lunch food out then."

Shayna nods her head in acknowledgement. "Thanks, so much love."

Shayna waits at noon outside the door of barracks ten for Albert.

Suddenly, Albert opens the main door. He's clutching a thick peanut butter sandwich and a large apple. He hands them both to Shayna.

"Sorry but this is all that I could get. They were watching me."

"Oh, thank you Albert, thank you so very much." Shayna grabs the sandwich and breaks it into three pieces. She urgently gobbles down her share and then takes two large bites out of the apple almost swallowing them whole. Albert watches her eat like a starved animal.

"Okay love, now I must go feed my mother and little brother." Shayna wipes her mouth with the back of her dirty hand like a street beggar and turns to go.

"Don't the guards bring food into your barracks?"

"No, not too much anymore, most of the women are starving and sick. Some are dead and frozen on the floor. Mom, Walter and I have to carry their bodies outside because the guards really don't care. We don't want dead bodies in our cell." Shayna remarks as if it were just another daily occurrence in the land of happenstance.

Albert stares at Shayna startled. She's institutionalized now, Albert deems. She thinks that dead bodies are just another piece of old furniture to be tossed out just like the Germans, just like that miserable scum, Jingo and Vujkovic.

"Okay, thanks again." Shayna waves goodbye to Albert as she turns to go. She clutches the food tightly in her hand and then hides it under her vest.

"We're getting out of here tonight, all of us." Albert declares.

"How? Where will we go?"

"It doesn't matter, we are leaving tonight!"

'We'll freeze to death out there."

"You're freezing and starving in here anyway."

Shayna glares at him in astonishment at the truth and grabs him for warmth. They hug briefly and Shayna steps back satisfied. "Walter has a really bad cold and my mother won't leave him behind."

"Convince her then. We all can escape together when it gets dark."

"I'll try, but if she won't come then I'll be here tonight by myself."

"Okay," Albert is adamant. "We'll go get help somewhere and come back for your mother, brother and my family too."

"Sounds like a plan!" Shayna smiles up big seeming to finally be filled with utter happiness. She then turns and runs toward the women's barracks, still hiding the food under her clothes.

CHAPTER TWENTY-FIVE

ALBERT SITS AT his banker's desk, turning around checking to make sure that he is alone. There are surprisingly no guards in sight, Albert notes to himself. They were all up drinking and partying last night so they must be hung over today. Jingo is the worst. I can never tell what mood he's in because he has a severe personality disorder. What a madman he is.

Albert opens a drawer and takes out a medium sized wooden box. He lifts the lid and in it are about one hundred diamonds of different sizes and colors. Albert hesitates, contemplating for a moment and then he lowers the lid and puts the box back into the drawer.

Do I really want to do this? Albert swivels in his chair. Yes, yes, I do because these murdering excuses for human beings are starving all the women and children to death. They are just human trash. Why do I care if I take their stolen diamonds to help Shayna and our families survive? We need to escape, or we will all die in this wretched, dismal death camp. God save us all.

Albert reopens the drawer and takes out the box of diamonds again. His eyes keep scanning at all times wondering who may be spying on him. He picks up a notebook, opens the pages and begins counting the diamonds and comparing them to his records. He erases some notes. Albert then glances around to make sure that he is not being watched as he secretly hides four of the largest diamonds in his fingers and secretly drops them into his pants pocket. He places the wooden box full of diamonds back into the drawer and closes the notebook. There done, he is shaking, but no guards are in sight to see it.

Shayna waits in the shadows for Albert outside of barracks ten. She wears a camp uniform, heavy military boots and has somehow managed to take a shower. Albert comes out of the door after work and Shayna whispers his name to the wind. "Psst, psst, Albert, Albert."

Albert hears her calling and immediately finds her. "Let's go. Let's get out of here. Now!"

"Thank God. Oh, thank God," Shayna whimpers wanting freedom as much as Albert. They gaze briefly at each other with easy familiarity and tenderness.

"I'll bribe the guards with a diamond and the others we will use for food and shelter on the outside."

"Diamonds?" Shayna tilts her head in a question of amazement, but then smiles happily just to be on her way out of the death trap.

Albert and Shayna slink up to the entrance gates of Banjica. A short Serbian guard awaits them. Albert speaks quietly with him while Shayna lingers in the shadows. Albert hands the short guard one diamond. The guard takes the diamond and holds it up to the camp light bulbs. "You sure this is the real thing? It looks like a piece of glass to me."

That's because you're a jerk that's never seen a real diamond in your life before you idiot, Albert reflects on the short guard's reluctance. "Sure, it's real, why would I risk my life for a piece of worthless glass?"

Hesitating and weighing his options, the guard finally smiles big with rotten teeth, looks over at Shayna and shakes his head no. He puts up two fingers like a grade school kid wanting teacher's approval. Stupid kid, Albert deliberates in his head.

"I want two diamonds, there are two of you." The short guard stomps out in defiance.

"But I don't have two diamonds, only one." Albert grins keeping his temper in check.

"Then I can only let you through the gate, not your friend in the shadows."

"What?" Albert dares the guard.

"Sorry, but I'm the gate keeper, my rules."

Albert glares at the guard in revulsion. So, this is Mother May I? What a silly clown.

"Well, where are they?" The clown demands.

Albert reluctantly hands him a second diamond. Albert then turns around and motions for Shayna to come to the gate. She quickly responds to Albert's request and slips cautiously out of the shadows. The gate guard silently opens the gate and both Albert and Shayna go through.

The gate closes behind them. They stand in awe looking at each other for a short time then cast their eyes around in foreboding.

A tall Serbian guard now stands in front of them with his hand out.

"What?" Albert declares, startled. "I already paid the other guard."

"I want paid too. This is a risk for us." The tall guard keeps his hand out in a begging position. "We could be shot for this."

"Get out of my way! A deal's a deal!" Albert is frantic by now and lets it loose.

The guard shakes his head no and stomps his heavy military boots in a threatening gesture. Boots, Albert remembers, I've had those things slammed into my stomach before.

The tall guard motions for the diamonds. "I want two diamonds, one for each of you." Albert falters a moment; his eyes scan Shayna for her reaction. She has none but is frozen in indecision. Albert looks away into the yawning silence of the night sky. The moon blasts its light on the tall guard's menacing face shining in its contortion and towering over them like a troll that just happened to appear from under a bridge demanding payment for crossing.

"Is there another guard or are you the last?" Albert acquiesces, a slave to survival.

"I'm the very last," the troll gargles. Albert and Shayna cast a deep melancholy look at each other before Albert hands the tall guard his last two diamonds. He pockets them but doesn't remove himself from Albert's path of exit. "Now back into the camp, Mr. Albert the Banker."

"What?" A shocked then pained expression spreads across Albert's face. "No, you get out of our way, a deal's a deal!"

The tall guard shakes his head no.

"I paid both of you two diamonds, now let us go! Where's your honor?" The tall guard starts to laugh.

The short guard opens the gate and comes through it. "Get back into the camp, both of you, now!"

"You bastards!" Albert spits out onto the pavement.

The tall guard continues to laugh. "Yea, that's what we are, bastards. Ha! Ha!"

The short guard breaks out in laughter too. "Now I can buy the best whores in the house."

"You thieving scum!" Albert is incensed.

The tall guard defends himself. "Scum? You're scum for stealing from the Fuhrer."

"The Fuhrer is a thief too."

"Watch your mouth."

"I didn't steal those diamonds. I brought them into the camp in the heels of my shoes."

The tall guard bends over in laughter. "Oh my God, Ha! Ha! Ha!"

Albert stays firm. "We want out of this hell hole! Screw the Fuhrer!" Albert pushes past the tall Serbian guard and motions for Shayna to follow him. "We've paid and now we're leaving!" The tall guard puts his rifle up to Albert's head.

Shayna blurts out, "Albert, I don't want you to die over this."

Albert throws both guards a bomb of loathing as if they had no other purpose in life except menace. The tall guard motions for Albert to move back through the gate and return to the camp as he continues to hold his rifle up to Albert's head. Shayna looks away as not to inflame the precarious circumstances.

"Albert, we can go back now. It's okay." Shayna is shaking.

Albert moves carefully back into the camp, followed by Shayna. The tall guard lowers his rifle from Albert's head but continues to follow him with the rifle through the scope. The short guard locks the gate behind them.

The short guard is flippant. "Next time, Mr. Albert the Banker, bring me some red rubies. My lady in the big house loves red. Ha! Ha! Ha!"

CHAPTER TWENTY-SIX

ALBERT SITS AT his desk in barracks number ten. There are no guards with him. Jingo walks in and closes the door behind him. "Mr. Banker, we need to talk." Jingo studies Albert with an assassin's eye.

"Yes, about what?" Albert plays it cool feigning indifference thinking that he might have over played his hand.

Jingo opens the palm of his hand and displays the four large diamonds. Albert glances at them and then looks away blank faced, trying to swallow the bitter taste that has come to his mouth.

"Why did you steal these diamonds?"

"Well, because there was no cash available."

"What?"

Albert shakes his head up and down in total and confirmed confidence, feigning a fearless and passive stare.

"Since when did you sign-up for-profit sharing?"

"I didn't." Albert speaks without facing him.

"What happened to all your happy horseshit about honesty and virtue?"

Albert looks down at the floor, not ashamed. *Survival you idiot,* Albert ponders to himself.

"I really don't want to tell the Commandant that we trusted the wrong banker. I will look like a moron for choosing you."

Albert searches in his head for a moment, "Okay; I will give you what you want to survive. What do you say to that?"

"Yes sir."

"So, you have been corrupted, "Right?"

Albert puts his hand over his mouth and closes his eyes. "Yes sir."

"Starting today, Albert the crooked banker, you will never be left alone again. You will always have guards watching you, every minute."

"Yes sir."

Jingo walks towards the closed door and turns around. "Say, Albert the Crook, don't let this happen again or you will have an unfortunate accident, Okay?"

Albert nods in acknowledgement.

CHAPTER TWENTY-SEVEN

SHAYNA WAITS BY the front door of barracks ten for Albert to come out. She is dressed in a regular camp uniform and heavy boots.

Jingo comes out and surprises her as she stands by the door. "What are you doing here again bothering Albert the Banker, getting him into trouble?"

Alarmed by this irritable man, Shayna takes a few steps backward, but he is in her face. Jingo's thin lips twist into a smirk and he studies Shayna with one eye closed.

Shayna thinks, *I remember you now from the women's barracks; you're the drunken bum that spit on the floor.* She keeps her tearing eyes away from him knowing that she doesn't have the strength to fight this monster with ten heads.

Jingo instinctively reads her and tenses up glaring at Shayna in belligerence. He narrows his eyes as if he remembers her too. She was the loudmouth challenging him in the women's barracks. Suddenly Jingo reaches out and grabs Shayna by the long, flowing brown hair.

"Let me go! Let me go!" Shayna lets out a shrill scream.

"Stay away from the banker, you pushy little bitch!"

"Get your hands off me! Stop!" Shayna jerks back convulsively and gives out a terrified, rattling shriek like she is being murdered. She inhales his putrid body odor and her empty stomach churns as if wanting to throw up what's not there.

"You need to be taught a lesson you loudmouth bitch, ha, ha."

Jingo attempts to drag Shayna behind the barracks by her hair. She screeches in terror as she alternatively falls to the ground and pulls herself up again.

"Shut up you little tramp! I'll do to you what I do to the rest of the nasty little bitches."

"You're drunk! Help!" Shayna shakes and gasps in total panic as her mind scrambles, racing with each jolt.

Jingo starts to rip off Shayna's clothes as she fights back by throwing punches and kicking. He slaps her across the face, and she falls to the ground. Jingo jumps on top of her, pinning her to the ground. He laughs, "Too late, you worthless little bitch."

Suddenly Murray appears and grabs Jingo, throwing him off of Shayna. Jingo rolls to the side.

"What the hell are you doing?" Murray screams red faced at Jingo.

"Teaching this little bitch a lesson."

"The Commandant does not allow this! It will cause the Jews to riot!"

Jingo glares at Murray, temporarily stopping. He narrows his eyes as he looks around for a witness. None are in sight and the thought of ignoring Murray seems to tempt him. Murray reads Jingo's body language which appears to say: 'It would be a fight to the finish with this old Jew'. Murray stares down tough, holding his own as Jingo mulls it over again.

"Leave now and I will take care of this." Murray feigns composure. "I will keep this quiet."

Jingo pinches up his face at Murray and shoots him a threatening arrow. "You'll get rid of this trouble making little bitch or I'll report her to Administrator Vujkovic. He'll take care of her alright. She'll be gone by tomorrow!"

Murray nods in confirmed acknowledgement. He stands in self-possession as if anything less would challenge and enflame the insane monster before him.

"Vujkovic will line her up in the firing squad with the rest of the nuisance bitches." Jingo finally relents, stands up shaking himself off and buttons up his pants.

"You will pay for this, someway, somehow!" Jingo threatens Shayna who still lies on the ground in tears. Jingo stomps back to the main courtyard and barrack ten.

Murray's eyes follow Jingo, as if he knows him through and through. Murray speaks out loud as Shayna is speechless, still face down on the ground. "This man will periodically just destroy someone's life for no reason. He's billions and billions of nothings... pure evil."

Bella and Murray stand alone and talk in the main courtyard.

Bella is near tears. "I know that Shayna was staying with the German Frolich in the back house."

Murray considers Bella's words carefully. "What can we do? She will be raped and executed if she stays here in the camp. No one can control her; she does whatever she wants just like the rest of the young wild animals here in this captured war zone."

Bella looks away. Tears fall while a dark honey kind of wise sounding voice speaks. "Oh Murray, I just feel so guilty, but I don't want her to suffer and die in this God forsaken prison. Her life has just begun."

Murray dips his head in a nonverbal conformity.

"Maybe she will go back to Officer Frolich's house again," Bella relents uneasily. Murray agrees in consenting accord.

"I'll talk to her." Bella wipes her tears as if maybe finding a reluctant but enduring solution.

"Fine with me Bella but keep it from Albert. If you don't, he will get himself killed for love. You know, Romeo and Juliette."

Bella guffaws. "It's survival first, then food and then love, in that order."

Murray laughs. "He will understand when he's older."

"They're both so young and so dumb."

It's late afternoon in front of barracks ten. Shayna moves back and forth as she hides in the shadows and craggy bushes near the barrack's front door. She is dressed in a man's camp uniform of drab pants, combat boots, an oversized shirt and her hair is cut short like a boy's. She serves her newfound masculinity well.

Power, rage and ruthlessness is Jingo's specialty as he slams out of the front door of barracks ten with his loud blistering sarcastic persona that he wears like a uniform. Shayna spots him and falls to the ground pinning herself down like a sniper. Jingo checks around for Shayna near the door, sees nothing and warily saunters away looking back periodically, hoping to catch of glimpse of her. Shayna lays in silence until Jingo is out of sight.

The cold, cruel facts of life in the camp finally hit her hard: steal or starve, hide or die, disappear or get raped. The rules of this game give her a blunt reflective slap across the face. Shayna tightens up in defeat and aggravation. *What happened to my young, carefree life?* She buries her head in her hands and sobs uncontrollably in the dry dirt. A small insect crawls near her eyes looking for moisture.

CHAPTER TWENTY-EIGHT

STILL **DRESSED IN** her male camp uniform, Shayna sits in the living room of Officer Frolich's house. Her short hair falls about her face. Shayna plays it cool, swallowing the humiliation of her bad choices and feigning with impressive conviction that everything is alright.

"I'm glad that you're back. I missed you," Frolich smiles trying to contain it all inside.

Shayna holds a vacant stare unmoved just like her combat boots that are propped up on his favorite foot stool.

"Such a clever girl you are, you could pass for a pretty young boy."

Shayna immediately snaps out of it, sprouts defiance and passes him a crass frown.

You've been out there way too long, Frolich deems to himself backing off.

Night brings darkness and deceptions as Albert and Murray talk in their bunk cell. "Have you seen Shayna lately?"

"No, I haven't." Murray responds.

"She didn't tell me where she was the last time that she disappeared."

"Albert, you know that it's very dangerous for a young girl to be hanging around outside in the camp, don't you?"

"She cut her hair, wears a man's uniform and looks like a boy now."

"It doesn't matter Albert! Some of these guards like young boys too." Albert rumples up his face like he just bit into a sour lemon and looks away.

Shayna finally gives up the macho attitude and dresses in a flowered house dress with a swirly pink ribbon in her short hair. It's as if she can change sexes like a snake sheds its skin. Officer Frolich sits near her on the sofa appearing to give off a body language of romantic insecurities. His face turns down into a clown's mask. "Do you actually like me Shayna?"

Shayna jumps back at the pitiful clown. "Of course, I do, but not with that bottled up terrified look on your face." Shayna moves uneasy in her seat and thinks, *I do like you Frolich, but I love my husband. I'm pretty sure I love my husband. I'm only nineteen years old so how can I know who I really love? So just quit with the insecurity stuff and I'll be okay.* Shayna manages a guarded smile for him, and he smiles back.

"Just checking," Wilhelm wonders out loud.

An awkward silence permeates until Officer Frolich blurts out. "Will you sleep with me tonight Shayna?"

"Why do you ask? You never asked when you kidnapped me!"

Wilhelm quietly bows his head either ashamed of his past behavior, or in love, or both.

Bella hides by the outside door of the woman's barracks meditating in the shifting night shadows. The air is cold but fresh and clean, relieving the deadening stench that permeates inside her barracks. Murray walks by and casually drops a brown paper sack near some bushes. Bella waits until Murray is gone, looks around to make sure that no one is watching and then goes out to discretely pick up the sack and hides it under her camp uniform. She then walks back up into her stifling overcrowded barracks.

Bella goes into her bedroom cell and motions to Walter. They secretly hide and share a peanut butter sandwich, piece by piece and chewing occasionally only when no one is looking.

Bella then motions to Stella and Sarah. They each in turn sit by Bella as she slips each one of them a peanut butter sandwich.

Though not at all sexually attracted to other boys, Wilhelm doesn't spend any time talking to girls either. Fearing that he won't make it to college, both his parents discourage him from dating. Thus, his days are spent in the library, in study hall or functioning as president of the Physics Club. He congregates with his fellow male academic social misfits. Despite the fact that he is physically attractive and from a well-off family, the girls seem to sense that Wilhelm is not available. They appear to accept that he is thoroughly taken by his scholastic ambitions. So, they turn their attention to a more accessible target for their hormonal frustrations, the pompous school athletes who mostly flip them around like pizza dough and burn the girls' crusts.

However, Wilhelm did go to his high school's sophomore formal with a girl from his class. When he tries to put his hands on her breasts during the opening dance, she cringes, slaps him in the face and runs crying into the restroom. After his date totally disappears from the gym, Wilhelm leaves the dance too, spending the remainder of the evening in a nearby park. Dressed in a tux, he endures giggles and taunts from the usual park night crew. He doesn't care. "I'll just go home at ten and tell my parents that I had a wonderful time," Wilhelm mutters out loud. The park crew finally just ignores him. Most of them are out of it by now on booze and sex-capades.

The next day in school the brother of his date for the formal dance, who just happens to be the same team captain that Wilhelm met on the soccer field, approaches him at his locker and threatens him.

"Keep your hands off my sister or I'll break every tooth out of your miserable head!" He screams at Wilhelm red faced with blue eyes bulging. All the students in the hallway suddenly become desperately quiet as Wilhelm's face falls, wilting like a hot cabbage leaf.

"You're a sick pervert! You ruined my sister's dance!" The team captain continues yelling as Wilhelm closes up his locker and pulls his fists together ready to strike. Deciding against that, he drags himself past the pointing hallway students. The team captain's intimidating eyes follow him as he ambles away. Laughs and jeers permeate the air.

The following week a girl that Wilhelm sits beside in study hall asks him to help her with her physics homework. Wilhelm smiles in flattery and moves his desk closer to hers, but instead of getting out her homework she whispers into Wilhelm's ear. "Do you know what I can use for a sex lubricant, maybe Vaseline?"

"Ah..." Wilhelm trips over his words pretending that he is experienced. "I... guess... so." Unable to read him, the girl smiles at Wilhelm like he's just confirmed a top sex secret. Later that day the same girl passes Wilhelm in the hallway and he reaches out, touching her buttocks. Astonished at his impropriety, she turns around and knocks the books out of Wilhelm's arms. He stands dumbfounded thinking that the girl had asked for the sexual advance. A few random boys come by and kick Wilhelm's books off down the hall forcing him to chase after and retrieve them.

When Wilhelm goes to study hall the next day, the same girl has now moved across the room and refuses to even make eye contact with him. After a few minutes into study hall a note arrives directing Wilhelm to go to the principal's office. As Wilhelm walks into the office he feels a sharp twinge run through his entire body. *What did I do?* He finds himself swept away with churning stomach acid.

"Sit down Mr. Frolich," the principal suggests.

"Okay." Wilhelm gives him an inquisitive grunt holding back his stomach fluid.

"Look Wilhelm, you're a sophomore in high school now and you should know better than to grab a girl's breasts or another girl's buttock."

"What?" Wilhelm pretends astonishment though not meeting the principal's eyes as he feels the nausea twisting in his gut.

"I've had two complaints about you now, one from the sophomore formal dance and another just recently from a girl saying that you grabbed her while she was walking down the hall."

Wilhelm stares over the desk at the principal with his mouth gaping open finally meeting the principal's eyes.

"I had to call your parents and if this continues, they will have to show up for a school meeting."

"But..."

"No buts or ahs, Wilhelm. There are witnesses confirming that you did it."

Wilhelm falls back into his chair and drops his books onto the floor but remains silent.

"Well, what do you have to say for yourself?"

Wilhelm shakes his head in disbelief lowering his head without a word and senses himself dropping into a self-imposed mental pit.

"Okay, then young Frolich, I guess that your parents will have to come to a meeting with us.

Finally relenting Wilhelm looks up, his face alert as the words come out flat and dull. "But... I thought that's what I'm supposed to do on a date."

"What? Who told you that?" The principal is dumbfounded.

"Ah... no one, sir... I just surmised it."

The principal lets out an unbelieving gasp trying to read the look on Wilhelm's face.

"Yes," Wilhelm shakes his head in the affirmative biting his upper lip. He wants nothing more than to run out of the office and go home.

"What about the girl in the hall? You know the one... she says that you grabbed her butt. You weren't on a date with her."

"Well sir, she asked me about sex, and I thought that it was an invitation to touch her."

The principal passes a deep sigh of resignation and folds his hands on his desk. "Look son, I don't know where you get your information and your parents need to teach you some sex education, but you just can't go around grabbing girls anytime that you feel the urge."

"What? No?"

"No! That's assault and battery. Both girls' parents complained about you touching their daughters sexually and they may want to press charges against you."

"But I... I... thought that the girls liked me."

"Well, maybe they did, but not anymore. You will have to learn some manners around girls."

Wilhelm hangs his head. "Yes sir. Will you teach me?"

The principal closes his eyes and falls back into his chair as if he's being hit with a bland, inoffensive joke.

CHAPTER TWENTY-NINE

SHAYNA AND OFFICER Wilhelm Frolich sit at the dining room table in his house and eat. Wilhelm reaches over and takes Shayna's hand. She smiles at him with a newfound comfort. "Wilhelm, I have something to ask you that is very important to me." Officer Frolich releases Shayna's hand and stares at her as if waiting for the sky to fall.

"Can my mother and brother come here to work, at something, anything?" The question falls like a torpedo as a discomforting silence suddenly fills the room.

"I'll think about it Shayna."

"They can possibly stay in one of the small bungalows behind the house, and maybe they can be servants of some sort."

"Well I don't know."

Shayna pulls away into a cloud of forced distance. Wilhelm turns away feeling blindsided then looks at his object of affection. He seems to melt as if his heart ached. "Well, does your mother talk a lot?"

"No, she hardly says anything at all." Shayna recovers with a stubborn flicker of hope.

"And your brother, he looks like a spoiled, big mouthed little brat."

"No, my mother will slap him down. She's a strong woman."

"Well Shayna, if someone reports that they are your relatives then, I just don't know."

Shayna pouts like a child and then catches herself, pushing the little girl away. "I must do something for them because they are my family." A grown woman appears fighting to emerge.

"So, my love, you must be very careful now. Remember that I'm an Aryan man and I will be forgiven, and you are a woman, German or Jewish, the firing squad awaits you."

With the injustice of it all sinking in, Shayna turns her head away like the rain may start falling any second now. "So... I will take the risk and you... you will think about it?"

"Yes, I will think about it."

"For how long?" Shayna begs as the rain disappears and the wind comes.

"Oh Shayna, you force me because you know that I'm so fond of you." An airy silence fills the room as the spark of Shayna's hope begins to take form.

Officer Frolich surrenders to his love. "We do need someone to shovel snow and clean the sidewalks back here, clear and plant a garden in the spring, and pull weeds."

Shayna gives out a cry of overdue relief. "Oh!"

"Can your mother and that little brat do that?"

Shayna nods yes and her new smile lights up the room. Wilhelm smiles back warily, still uneasy with his risky decision.

"I'll have Mimi take my mother a note."

"What? Absolutely not! No notes at all! Do you understand that a note is evidence?" Shayna covers her mouth with her hands and then her face in an impending fear.

"If a note is found all of you will die, even Mimi."

A sudden shot of panic shakes her as she gathers herself up. She releases a long drawn out, heavy breath. "Okay then. I will have Mimi tell her with a whisper to come here with Walter to see me in secret, maybe as a friend of Mimi's just visiting."

"Late at night, say three in the morning and very quietly with no luggage."

"Okay Wilhelm. I'm so happy."

"If that little kid talks loud or creates a commotion, I will have no say at all in what will happen to them and maybe to you, too."

"I'll tell Mimi to have Walter gagged."

Officer Frolich glowers at Shayna in apprehension and rolls his eyes in reflection. *What have I done now for this woman? God help me.*

In the early dark of the evening Mimi enters the woman's barracks and leisurely checks around asking a few women for Bella Weinberg's whereabouts. A Slavic woman points to Bella's unit and Mimi calmly goes in.

"I'm looking for Bella Weinberg."

A Slavic woman in an adjacent bed points to Bella. Bella looks up in surprise. "Oh, Hi."

"Hi Bella," Mimi smiles in recognition as if she has known Bella for years effecting the secret. "Yes, I'm Bella Weinberg," she speaks softly under her breath nodding and smiling.

Mimi whispers something into Bella's ear. Bella shakes her head up and down again in a cut and dry comprehension. Mimi then prepares to leave.

"Bella, it's so nice to see you again my dear friend. Your husband just wanted me to say 'hi' and that he still loves you." Mimi grins and waves like a dear old friend just passing blessings along. Mimi turns to walk away.

Bella waves back beaming. "Thank you so much. That makes me so very happy to hear. I

miss my husband so much."

CHAPTER THIRTY

MURRAY REPEATEDLY CHECKS the electrical fence in front of number five, the Gypsy barracks. A red light is on in a small iron cage which signals that the electricity is in fact still on.

In the darkest of night, without a sound Bella and Walter amble on insect feet to the back of the prisoner's barracks and wait by the locked gate of the chain-link fence. Like the house ghost, Mimi faintly appears in the foggy distance tiptoeing up to them. The ghost then glances up at the back guard stand and no one is stirring meaning that the guard is probably, as usual asleep by three a.m. She then carefully unlocks the gate and Bella and Walter come through as Mimi turns and locks the gate behind them again. Mimi motions for them to quietly follow her as they head to a row of three small servant bungalows behind the main house. Mimi opens the door of the middle bungalow and Bella and Walter go in first.

The servant's quarters are a small studio of one room, a miniscule kitchen and an even smaller bathroom is off to the side. It's a shack in comparison of what Walter is accustomed to and he turns up his nose like a disgusted cartoon character. Walter removes the scarf tied around his mouth which prevents him from talking. "I'm gonna live in this cereal box?"

Bella gives him a conk upside his head. "Go sit in a chair and put that gag back on, now!" Walter finds a small sofa and sits down tying the scarf back around his dangerous mouth.

Mimi shakes her head at Walter as if he was an ungrateful changeling sent to torment her. Suddenly Shayna appears. Mimi nods to her and then leaves.

Shayna hugs Bella. "Mother I'm so glad to see you both. I've missed you so much."

Walter removes the scarf from his mouth again and jumps up to hug Shayna. "Shayna, Shayna, my long-lost sister." Shayna hugs him back and then pushes him away like a poison toad trying to kiss her.

"Please Mother, if Walter talks loud or causes any kind of trouble at all, we all risk being killed. You and Walter are here in secret and if Jingo finds out about this then we'll all be taken to the firing squad."

"Alright, alright, I understand." Bella confirms anxiously holding on to her composure.

"You must keep Walter absolutely quiet at all times, at all times! Okay?"

Bella glares into Shayna's eyes pushing back her own fright, and then turns to Walter. "Do you hear that Walter, not a sound, okay? Quiet!"

Walter squints up in the light and rattles his head in a yes motion. "Can I play outside?"

"Once in a while Walter," Shayna directs, "but you must do something like rake the leaves or haul trash."

"I'm a trash picker now?" Walter bursts out like a little school boy.

Shayna starts to tear. "Oh Mom, with Walter around, we'll all be shot."

"Please Shayna, you can't cry now."

Shayna wipes the tears from her face with the back of her hand. "Okay mother, you and Walter will be snow maintenance and you will, ah, you will never, well, speak to me nor act like you know me."

Not thinking, Bella's face suddenly falls in pain and astonishment.

"The German Security Officer has papers saying that I'm a German woman, if need be."

Bella gapes at Shayna shocked again, but then gathers her composure. "Oh, I see, then fine."

"I must respect this, or we will all face the firing squad, we will be shot!"

"Yes, I know Shayna, yes I know!"

Fresh beads of stress begin to form on Shayna's forehead. "These are the servant's quarters. You will find everything that you need in here because I prepared it for you."

"Yes, and thank you darling daughter."

"If you need anything, you will ask Mimi, the woman that let you in. She lives next door to you, okay?"

"Shayna you are only nineteen years old and you have done all this, so don't feel badly that Walter and I have to live in hiding like this. We both love you very much."

"Okay Mother." Shayna finally gives up a big smile.

"Please just go now. Dad is alright and Albert and all his relatives are okay too, for now."

"Fine Mother, just fine."

Shayna leaves and softly shuts the door behind her. She walks up to the back door of Officer Frolich's house and only looks back once.

CHAPTER THIRTY-ONE

APPROXIMATELY ONE HUNDRED civilian male prisoners line up in two rows in the main courtyard. Armed Serbian State guards surround them. Two large open military trucks park in the distance ready to deliver them to their work destinations, some to their deaths.

One Serbian guard yells his orders at the prisoners. "Attention! All able-bodied men will be shipped out tomorrow to the Semlin Sajmiste camp near Belgrade." The prisoners shudder in fear and anxiety, talking among themselves.

The next morning the two open trucks pull up into the main courtyard. The hundred men divide into groups of fifty each and get onto the two trucks. Minutes later the two trucks, full of apprehensive, sad civilian inmates disappear into the distance.

The sun rises again on the women's barracks. Most of the women starve to feed their children. They know that their men are gone, but there is so little life left in them that some appear walking bones. The newer women residents often fight with the previous ones as the horrendous stress of overcrowding, no food, and appalling sanitary conditions rule like an invisible demon, and the intense cold lingers on. The barracks is never properly sanitized or even cleaned. Clutter, blood, vomit and dirty blankets litter everywhere with the foul, permeating smell of the plugged, overflowing latrines.

Some older women sit out in the cold night praying for death, hoping that it will take them without a fight. Some lay still and frozen to death on the straw floors of the barracks. Children are so thin and sunken in that they don't even look human anymore.

CHAPTER THIRTY-TWO

MURRAY WAITS FOR Sarah outside of the women's barracks. He discreetly slips a brown paper sack full of peanut butter sandwiches and a large bottle of clean water to her without being seen. She hides them under her filthy clothes and goes back into the stench of the barracks. Sitting on the bed, Sarah secretly shares the food with her own and Stella's family. As the sandwich sack holding only crumbs falls to the floor, a rat appears from under the bed and drags it beneath the fallen covers.

The next night as Sarah waits for Murray and the food, she spies an old Jewish woman sitting outside on a rock in the cold snow. *That old lady could be my great grandmother,* she reflects to herself. Bending down Sarah catches a light on the old lady's withered, opaque eyes. *You're blind,* Sarah thinks, *probably cataracts.* Sensing that someone is near, the old lady jerks in alarm.

"Don't worry Grandma, no one will hurt you." The old lady relaxes a bit and lets out a cough of rising steamy air. Age had hit her hard with cracked skin, no teeth, frail bones and the absence of sight. "Where is your family?" Sarah asks her in a shivering whisper.

"Dead," The senior lets the word flitter out and rise up to a place where she hopes to be soon. The old lady falls off the rock in front of Sarah and now lays prone in the freezing snow.

I've entered a death ritual, Sarah realizes. Should I help her get back into the barracks or should I just let God take her up to be with her family? The old woman's eyes close with a sigh of long-awaited relief.

"Grandma," Sarah tries to help the senior to her feet by hoisting her up by the shoulders, but the old woman pushes Sarah's hands away and whimpers a tone of intense agitation. Sarah stands

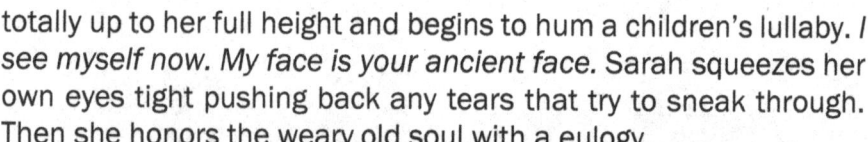

totally up to her full height and begins to hum a children's lullaby. *I see myself now. My face is your ancient face.* Sarah squeezes her own eyes tight pushing back any tears that try to sneak through. Then she honors the weary old soul with a eulogy.

"God bless you Grandma, and may you reach heaven tonight with happiness despite your suffering. I know that there is no hate left in your pure heart and you have forgotten the evil ones who will eventually die just like you. Ashes to ashes that the wind will blow away somewhere into eternity. All is vanity. "

Two weeks later a signpost on the outside of the women's barracks which reads: 'QUARANTINE – Influenza & Typhoid epidemic – contagious – no admittance.'

Everyone is ill with coughs, spitting and moaning. Most of the children are already dead. Sarah and Stella share two twin beds pushed together with their three children by their sides. All are desperately ill and lay like downed cattle waiting for the mercy of slaughter.

Sarah does her best to speak. "This is... on purpose. They are... starving us... on purpose." Stella looks at her children as they lie silent. "The children... are dying... God save... us all." The two women weep in a religious union over their children, praying to God for mercy.

Murray appears in the women's barracks at 3:00 a.m., secretly hiding near their bed a sack of peanut butter sandwiches and a big water bottle for Sarah and Stella. He has a medical mask on, and rubber gloves cover his hands. Hardly able to move their emaciated bodies, the women can only turn their eyes up at him with a spiritual longing that somehow says, 'God will relieve us soon.' Murray's eyes fill with tears as he leaves the barracks.

The two urgently ill women somehow find the strength to get up and retrieve the sack. They feed themselves first and then attempt to give food and water to their children, but the children refuse to eat. They force water into their children's mouths, but they are mostly unresponsive. The water only flows to the side of the children's faces and spills onto the debris which contaminates the floor. Both women fall into their beds, holding their children and weeping in the relinquishments of last resort knowing that time is slipping away from them.

Two weeks later, two hundred dead women and children's bodies lay everywhere. Male prisoners without any medical masks or clothing protections cough and hold their noses from the rank odor as they carry the bodies out and dump them into a large waiting open military truck. Albert and Murray stand and watch.

"Do you see Sarah or Stella's bodies?" Albert is in tears with the overwhelming grief. "No, the bodies are so frozen and dark that they all look alike."

Albert shudders wiping his eyes with a handkerchief.

"Look Albert, sometimes it's just not good to watch such, such horrible things."

"I can't take this anymore!"

"Albert let's just go back to our barracks. I can't watch this either."

"Now my two nephews and my niece are dead. My whole family is gone... dead."

"I'm so sorry Albert. If I could blow this place up, I would do it, now!"

"Where are they taking them?"

"Their bodies will be burned outside of Belgrade, in the shooting ranges."

Albert gasps in horror.

"Albert... I hate this hell hole too."

Albert turns in circles as if he was casting a spell and screams at the Serbian guards who are watching the prisoners load the bodies. "You did this on purpose! You put all the women and children together so that they would get sick and die. Didn't you?"

The first Serbian guard steps forward stone faced and blasts a malicious grimace down on Albert as if giving it his best shot to control a madman. Albert stops the circles abruptly and shoots the guards a fierce evil glare of his own. "There are other barracks open! You starved them on purpose. You're filthy, dirty, little roaches!"

Murray grabs Albert by the shoulders and forcefully leads him away towards their barracks. A low resentful rumble leaves Albert's throat. "You low life bastards! You murdering scum!" The guards linger scrutinizing Albert as Murray continues to lead him away from the death scene.

"You're going to take a few days off from work. I'll talk to Jingo about this."

Albert is gasping for breath and holds his chest. "Where are Bella and Walter? Did you see their bodies anywhere?"

Murray shivers with concerned helplessness motioning no. "I'd like to scream too Albert, but what good would it do? They would just eliminate and replace me."

Albert falls to the ground in gripping, emotional pain and looks up at Murray like a lost child.

Bella and Walter shovel snow off of the walkways near the back house and the gate. They dress in heavy winter coats and gloves with scarves covering their faces. They are silent and have no identity except as house servants.

CHAPTER THIRTY-THREE

IN THE DEAD of night, Murray checks the three lines of electrical barbwire fence near the number five Gypsy barracks. The red light continues to signal active electricity.

Seven young Gypsy men come outside; a man named Pavel seems to be their leader. No guards are in sight so they can all talk freely.

"We want out of this prison cell." Pavel demands of Murray as if Murray had a magical wand to whisk him and his crew away.

"Yea, well, so do I," Murray agrees.

"So, then let's all make our escape together, just turn off the electrical charge, right now!" Murray looks at Pavel like he's crazy and attempts to exit the harrowing conversation. The other young Gypsies surround Murray.

"This is Ivan, my right-hand man." Pavel coolly announces to Murray as though they already have an agreement waiting in the wings. Ivan steps forward flexing his muscles like the world is watching. Murray looks into the bravado of Ivan and rolls his eyes, bored again, *I only see a young kid with a bone to pick,* Murray reflects to himself.

Ivan glowers into Murray's face. "You'll make an escape deal with us or your throat will be slit along with that crazy banker friend of yours. No one will give a shit, and you'll both just be replaced by someone else."

Murray deliberates briefly as various scenarios race through his head. "I, I don't know, I just don't know."

"You're afraid!" Ivan laughs at Murray's stuttering indecision.

"Of course, I'm afraid! To be afraid is a natural warning to be careful!"

Ivan sneers at Murray as though Murray believes that he has all the answers.

"I'm always afraid of the electricity and I must respect that fear or I will make a mistake and be electrocuted."

Pavel nods in agreement.

"You're a Jew, and you Jewish elders control this camp at the sacrifices of your own people," Ivan bounces back.

"If I don't do it, I'll be shot and someone else will stand up and take my place, just like you said," *you childish bore,* Murray thinks.

"You're a German stooge!" Ivan utters in distaste as he spits on the ground and bunches up his fists ready to strike, as if tempting Murray into a violent altercation.

Murray looks down at Ivan's spit slithering on the ground, fed up with the nonsense. "My responsibility is to save the Jews that can be saved and the others, beyond my control, will unfortunately die. I'm not God."

Ivan pinches up his face at Murray as though completely deflated by Murray's controlled response. "What about us Gypsies?" His fists are still clenched.

Pavel steps forward and breaks up the impending blows. "Stand back Ivan, we didn't meet this Jew here to argue over his role in the camp." Pavel lifts up his open hands at Ivan calming down the wild beast. Ivan dumbfounded relents like a robot attack dog.

"Well what is it then, Pavel?" Murray is beyond bored with Ivan's immature violence.

"Turn off the electricity by our barracks one night this week."

Murray hesitates in questionable acknowledgement. "What about the guards?"

Pavel regards all options having done his homework. "There are five armed guards on the watch towers, one on each corner of the camp in front, two on the sides and one in back."

Murray shakes his head affirmatively.

"Our barracks sits in the middle of two guards, a front corner guard and a side guard."

"Right," Murray agrees.

"We've checked the guards about three o'clock in the morning and most of them are halfway dozed off by then."

"Right again, but what exactly is it that you want me to do?"

"Just cut the electricity off for two hours, you know, and just walk away."

"I can only cut the electricity for one hour because I make my rounds once an hour at night and I must catch it!"

Ivan jumps into the conversation uninvited, "He said two hours!"

Murray slumps as if defeated. "Then just kill me now because the Commandant will execute me for this."

Pavel gives Ivan the signal to back off. "So, how will you explain the electrical short?"

Wrinkles of concentration spread from the corners of Murray's eyes. "Well, I can make it look like rats chewed through the wires." Murray imagines out loud. "The camp is full of them, everywhere."

Pavel and Ivan look at each other and strain their eyes in possible expectations.

"Fine," Pavel consents. "Just let us think about this for a couple of days. We will contact you for the exact night."

Murray agrees with a dip of his head but then evaluates the situation, *Oh my God, these are dangerous silly young men,* he broods as he walks away feeling Ivan's knife pointing at his back.

CHAPTER THIRTY-FOUR

ALBERT SLEEPS ON a twin bed in his cell. Murray walks in and Albert wakes up intuitively.

"Albert, it's been three days now since they took away the dead bodies, God bless their souls, but you must go back to work soon."

"I don't know if I can do it, again and again, tick, tick, tick. I got the craps too."

"Albert, you have to go back to work, or they will kill you for being useless."

Albert heaves a deep sigh, turns over and goes back to sleep.

Albert sits at his desk and launders money, items and real estate as usual. Two German guards watch his every move as ordered by Jingo. He turns around and glances at the guards and remembers, *I hate this place and will find a way out. I promise myself this. I will do everything in my dead family's honor to escape, God Bless their souls.*

CHAPTER THIRTY-FIVE

IN THE EARLY morning air ten Serbian guards and two German guards stand in front of Jingo in the main courtyard. Albert walks up and watches summing up personally, *There is something disturbingly childish about Jingo, like a sadistic little schoolboy peering out from behind wrinkled adult eyes and still pulling the wings off of flies. It's almost impossible to have a sane conversation with him for any length of time.*

"Bring out all twenty of the partisan rebels!" Jingo orders the guards. They run off at his service like a pack of baying hounds yelping at their master's command.

The ten guards storm into barracks number four where the Yugoslav partisans are housed. Some of the rebels are sleeping while others are awake taking a shower. Most of the rebels are skinny and weak from no food. They are nearing skeletal state.

The Serbian guards rouse the sleeping rebels and order them to dress immediately. The showering rebels are pulled from the showers with the water still flowing. Some of the rebels limp as they walk and attempt to dress themselves. The guards shove and attack in their unrelenting eagerness to make show and rise in rank.

The first Serbian guard yells orders. "You will now be taken to the main courtyard!"

A dressed young rebel yells back at him. "What's going on? You gave us no warning! What the hell is this?"

Another Serbian guard grabs the young rebel and pushes him toward the door, then threatens his life with a rifle barrel. Other Serbian guards point their rifles at the remaining rebels as all twenty Yugoslav rebels are herded out the barracks door.

The prisoners stand in front of the ten Serbian guards in the main courtyard. A small open military truck drives up and parks.

"All of you scum rebels will now get into the truck." Jingo screams unrelentingly, "Raus!" The rebels limp onto the small truck. Their rumpled clothes have an ill fitted look of poverty and broken spirit. Ten armed Serbian guards get into the open truck with them and hold the rebels at gunpoint.

"Should we tie them up?" One guard yells out to Jingo.

Jingo makes the call and laughs with allegiance to no one but himself. "Most of them are half dead already but tie them up if you think that you can't handle the bastards."

The second guard lingers for a moment and thinks, then he stares at the first guard and they both throw up their hands somewhat intimidated at Jingo's direct affront to the question of their macho strength and power. Both guards snicker and laugh at the tattered rebels and motion for the two German guards to get into the truck and drive.

With surprising agility Albert suddenly jumps up onto the truck with the rebels. "I'm going too!" Albert's eyes are finally singing with a newfound freedom of retaliatory justice and anticipation.

Jingo's brow falls in consternation. "Get off the truck Albert the Banker!"

Albert shakes his head no.

"Guards, throw that man off the truck, now!"

"I'm staying on the truck!" Albert is defiant.

"So, you quit your banking job today?"

Albert scowls in retaliation. "Yea and I just joined the Yugoslav partisan rebels."

A deep growl creases Jingo's face as his thin mouth draws into a straight line.

"I'm sick to death of that boring, stifling banking office and the miserable, horrible people in it!"

Jingo wavers in hatred, motioning the guards to throw Albert off the truck. Two guards grab Albert and attempt to throw him from the open truck. He latches onto a metal bar and two other guards have to join forces to pull him free. *There's a terrorist in there somewhere,* Jingo sums Albert up mentally. After struggling, screaming and fighting, Albert is finally dumped off the truck and onto the ground, landing out of air as he gasps and spits out his hatred.

Jingo gives the signal and the two German guards start the truck, driving it off rumbling and smoking. Jingo watches the truck as it disappears into the distance, its smoke leaving a desolate trail. He then looks over at Albert still on the ground. "Go back to work Albert the Banker, terrorist in the making."

CHAPTER THIRTY-SIX

THE REBELS SEE the truck is heading to the firing ranges on the outskirts of Belgrade where executions are enforced. They glower at the Serbian guards with open hatred in their weary eyes. As the rebels stare at the guards and each other, a surge of adrenaline seems to spark through them. They now appear to grip the sides of the truck with a newfound fear of death. As their hearts pump blood through their bodies, they fall in line at a disturbing attention.

The Serbian guards, lulled by the road trip, relax their grips on their rifles as their minds seem to wander into their skewed individual worlds and everyday problems which are not left unnoticed by the young partisan rebel. *Most of these guards don't appear to be trained military men nor have any military background. They look to only be opportunists recruited off the streets, possibly because of their lack of education, skills or trades. Some are even drifting off into the scenery, perhaps wondering how they are going to spend their mercenary money for killing us,* the rebel surmises, calculating the situation up completely and in its repugnant entirety. He gains eye contact with all the other rebels and secretly gives them a hand signal.

Suddenly, the truck hits a large pothole in the dirt road. The young rebel takes advantage of the sudden truck confusion and jumps on top of the first Serbian guard. The other rebels follow suit and attack the other nine Serbian guards with a newfound life or death survival instinct.

A mass brawl ensues in the back of the truck as chaos gains the upper hand. Heavy rifle shots fire loud and indiscriminately. It takes a few minutes for the two German guards driving the truck to realize what has happened. The truck comes to a noisy shudder and subsequent halt as the two guards get out of the truck's cabin and aim their rifles. The first German guard takes a bullet and falls to the ground before he can fire. The rebels on the ground band together and turn the small truck over on top of the second German guard pinning him underneath.

Mass anarchy and loud rifle shots ensue. Then a complete and eerie silence falls on the desolate scene. Dead men lay on the ground everywhere. The young rebel stands breathing out of the skin on his protruding ribs as his torn shirt blows in the breeze.

Several rebels pick up the dropped rifles, help a few wounded rebels to their feet, survey the situation briefly making sure that all the Serbian and German guards are dead and then run off into the distant woods without another word.

CHAPTER THIRTY-SEVEN

IN BARRACKS TEN, commandant of Banjica German Official Willie Friedrich and the Serbian Administrator of Banjica, Svetozar Vujkovic, meet at an official table with Jingo. They all dress in appropriate military uniforms according to their rank.

Willie Friedrich is enraged. "This level of incompetence will not be tolerated again! Is that clear Administrator Vujkovic?"

"Yes sir, Commandant Friedrich." Vujkovic sits up at extreme attention and trembles his feet underneath the table. The table shakes and Friedrich crinkles up his face in annoyance.

"You will take all measures to insure complete security, at all times! Is that understood?"

Vujkovic responds respectfully. "What do you suggest, Herr Commandant?"

"All captured war resistance rebels will be shot immediately upon coming into this camp!"

"Yes sir!" Vujkovic shows no hesitation in carrying out such an order.

Jingo also accepts the orders without a flicker of discernment as well.

"Twenty half dead partisans were too much for your sissy ten guards to handle!"

Vujkovic looks away intimidated, but then turns to the Commandant and repeats emphatically, "Yes sir!"

Commandant Friedrich pounds his fists on the table and snorts clearing his head as his coffee cup crashes to the floor.

Only giving the broken cup a passing glance, Vujkovic presses forward. "Let's just keep this unfortunate incident under cover and quiet. We can recruit some new Serbian State guards to replace the ones that were killed."

Commandant Friedrich nostrils flare in total rage at Vujkovic like a bull aiming to charge. Vujkovick pulls back with a clown face like he's ready to start juggling at any moment.

"You two are making me look like an idiot." The Commandant blares to Vujkovic and Jingo.

Jingo turns away in silence and private shame. *Everything is that fool Vujkovic's fault, he gave me the orders and now I have to take the blame too,* Jingo reflects in a sad secret whimper as if his faulty judgment had nothing to do with the partisan revolt. *If I can get Vujkovic out of the way, maybe with an unfortunate accident, then I can be camp administrator.*

The Commandant stands up ready to leave in his pompous atmosphere of picture-perfect decorum, furtively withered beneath the harsh light of reality.

After the Commandant leaves, Jingo and Administrator Vujkovic remain seated at the table contemplating what to do next that would appease the Commandant. Conform, compete and spy on each other is the rule as the balance of power shifts at a moment's notice and Vujkiovic makes an irritating attempt to reclaim it as he glares at Jingo. "This was all your fault. You gave the orders to your guards, not me."

"You bastard, you're always looking for something to complain about." Jingo snarls back at Vujkovic as the level of frustration increases.

"I wasn't even there; it was your call and now the Commandant blames me for your stupidity." Vujkovic spits out to make matters worse utterly consumed by his own egotistical importance.

"I'm not a human dartboard. You can't blame me for everything." A grimace of resentment crosses Jingo's face as he tinkers with his belt knife on the sly.

In a moment of bitter insults Vujkovic rises up out of his seat and attempts to grab Jingo by the throat. Jingo pulls out his knife and plants it in Vujkovic's face. Feeling besieged on all fronts, Vujkovic pushes Jingo's knife hand away and relents, turns around and stomps away.

Wilhelm's grandmother is in her early seventies with early onset dementia. She is confined to a bed in the den near a convenient bathroom and the kitchen. Although his mother is on leave from her high school teaching job, and very attentive to her own mother, the task of caring for the older lady both day and night exasperates her to the point of exhaustion. In addition, Wilhelm's father is now overloaded at his job too and often doesn't come home until midnight, making his help a moot point.

Wilhelm's own dog and cat that had wandered to his house as strays are enough for him to care for and go to school both. Wilhelm finds himself many times before or after school helping his mother out because she often is fast asleep on the sofa. At times Grandma has a restless night and must be tied down because she gets up and rambles outside into the street or gets lost in the woods.

To remedy this stressful situation Wilhelm's parents, hire a practical nurse that is only about ten years older than Wilhelm. Yet, only in her mid-twenties, this young girl is so very meticulous about caring for Grandma that she is favored over the other applicants. She is hired immediately because Grandma seems to like her the best. Mrs. Frolich could go back to work now, and this leaves Wilhelm at the mercy of this young house nurse who stays in the spare bedroom with her own bath and mini kitchen. She spends what little free time she has when Mr. and Mrs. Frolich are gone, and Grandma is asleep, putting her hands-on Wilhelm's crotch.

Wilhelm would take his pants off and leave his underwear on just in case one of his parents would suddenly appear at the door. He could then jump into his trousers in a split second pretending pure innocence. Judith the nurse would sometimes just rub Wilhelm's privates or if he was lucky, he would get to fondle her breasts, but they never have full on sex for whatever reason that Judith sees fit and proper behavior for her. Wilhelm never, ever objects to her advances but considers himself fortunate just to learn about sex. *God know the girls at school are off limits for me. They'll have me arrested if I even look at their breasts;* he recalls still sweating the unfortunate incidents with the school principal. *What a depressing thought that is.*

Wilhelm puts all that out of his mind as Nurse Judith continues to pet him into a sexual frenzy. He never had a girlfriend like this before and it's all such a glorious new thing for him to enjoy in fabulous secret which makes the sex even more tantalizing. Whenever Mrs. or Mr. Frolich is at home both Nurse Judith and Wilhelm feign boredom around each other. But when his parents leave the house all pandemonium breaks loose. Inadvertently Judith gives Wilhelm a hand job on the living room sofa in plain sight of Grandma who is in the den. The old lady almost faints gasping for air and howls so loud that the dog joins in outside in his doghouse forcing the cat to scramble and hide under a chair. Grandma forgets all about it by the time his mother comes home. Wilhelm has to clean his semen off the sofa afterwards with soap and a brush telling his mother that he spilt food on the spot. The two tricksters laugh for days over this dicey voyeuristic episode and Wilhelm never knew such fun before in his entire life.

This tryst goes on for about three months until one day Nurse Judith just fails to return from the grocery store. She doesn't show up at all the next day or the entire following week and Mrs. Frolich is more than agitated. She has to take another leave of absence from work again to find a new nurse. Wilhelm misses Judith the most but discovers himself now taking care of his own needs like a grown man instead of constantly searching for a girl to do the job for him. *Finally, I get it... what the boys mean when they talk about jerking off.* Wilhelm smirks to himself hardly believing his newfound awareness and sneaky hobby. A few more nurses come and go, but most of them are really old or married and choose to ignore Wilhelm's blooming manhood, so he stays in his room most of the time doing his homework, looking at pictures of naked women and stopping occasionally for self-induced sex breaks.

CHAPTER THIRTY-EIGHT

SHAYNA AND OFFICER Wilhelm Frolich sit in their living room area eating lunch. "I hardly see my mother and brother; it's like they're not even here at all."

"Great thing that is."

"So, Wilhelm, when will this war be over? I'd like to talk to my family again."

"Good question, I certainly don't know. I'd like to go live with my parents too; they're getting older now."

A fresh wash of tears begins to cover Shayna's face.

"What's the matter, love?"

"I don't know, I just don't really know."

"You know that I'm a single man Shayna." She gives him a query through her tears. "It's funny how things sometimes turn out."

Shayna intently waits in nervous anticipation.

"I thought that you and I would just be a sex fling and... "

"What?" Shayna interrupts.

"Yes, and that we would fight and argue and that you would just stay in the camp, angry and annoyed with me."

Shayna looks away as if remembering the hardships in the camp and not wanting to think about it.

"Now I look forward to seeing you every day, and the fact is, well, I think about you all day when I'm in that horrible place and I can't wait to come home to see you." Wilhelm stutters nervously stumbling and stammering over his words.

Shayna looks at him in surprise, reflecting that it's so out of character for him to stutter. "Shayna, I think that, I think that, I'm in love with you." *Well that's finally out now*, Wilhelm thinks heaving out a long pent up sigh as if blindly and deliriously happy with Shayna.

Shayna pulls away confused." What are we going to do? Tell me, what will happen to us locked away in this prison?"

"I don't know Shayna. I honestly don't really know."

Shayna's eyes water again.

"Look, we are safe here for now and your family's safe, at least for now. So, please stop crying. You make me feel as though I've done something to hurt you."

Shayna wipes her tears and glares at Wilhelm believing absolutely that *he has hurt me* and finally coming to terms with the 'delusional fantasies that adults tell themselves'.

Officer Frolich gazes at Shayna and creases his forehead chafed by his stiff collar, his leather boots and his war-torn circumstances.

CHAPTER THIRTY-NINE

IN THE COOL of the night air Murray talks with the young Gypsies Pavel and Ivan again in front of the number five Gypsy barracks. The other young Gypsies stand around them and listen intently. There are no guards in sight so they can talk freely. Murray asks, "How can you just leave your families and desert them here at Banjica?"

"These people aren't our families," Pavel divulges. "We just met them on the truck coming here."

Ivan blurts out in his usual fashion. "All of our families were killed by the Germans, murdered for no reason, executed!"

Murray closes his eyes in spiritual respect, "so very sorry to hear that Ivan." There is a silent moment of reverence as Murray reveals his true leadership qualities.

"Thank you." Pavel nods, being a gentleman.

"May God guide them." Ivan throws in unexpectedly out of character.

"So, Murray," Pavel moves forward. "We've all decided to do this tomorrow night, between three and four in the morning."

Murray acknowledges them with a head shake. "The electricity will be turned off from three a.m. to four a.m. and absolutely no longer. You will know the time because the red light will be off, understand?"

"Yes, we do." Pavel confirms.

Ivan verifies nonverbally in agreement.

"If you are not out by four a.m. tomorrow night, then I will repair the wire and turn the electricity back on anyway, okay? Is that understood completely and by everyone involved?"

Chapter Thirty-eight

Pavel and Ivan nod together again in total acknowledgement.

''If you are caught by the guards, I will deny you and won't help you. You will be immediately executed.'' Murray is adamant.

"Yes agreed," Pavel reiterates. "Ivan, do you agree with the execution risks?"

Ivan is quick to answer. "Yes, for me again." Ivan turns and looks at the other young Gypsies. They all acknowledge the agreement in its harsh reality.

CHAPTER FORTY

SHAYNA AND OFFICER Frolich eat dinner in the dining area. Mimi serves them.

"Will that be all sir?" Mimi is a trained and skilled server and Officer Frolich always treats her with the utmost respect. "Yes, thank you Mimi."

Mimi leaves the room and Officer Frolich's attention now turns to the detached, edgy Shayna as she stares straight ahead and ignores him. "Shayna, what's wrong with you?"

"Oh, don't you know? Don't you know?"

"No, no I don't know!"

"I'm pregnant."

Officer Frolich closes his eyes at the expected shock, but somehow having intuitively sensed it all along. *Well, I guess those rubbers don't work sometimes,* he remembers the warnings.

Shayna falls into a depression. "What am I going to do now?"

"I don't know." Frolich stammers as Shayna starts to cry. "Well, we'll just have a baby in private. Mimi can help you deliver."

"Life is just so difficult now," Shayna weeps. "It was all so easy before. Now every day is a struggle just to survive."

"Don't cry love, I'm happy."

Shayna wipes her tears now knowing that their similarities erase their differences of ethnicity, religion and culture.

"We can go live with my parents in Landshut. They always wanted grandchildren anyway." Shayna heaves a sigh of encouraging relief giving out a cough of laughter among the tears. However, she still holds onto her doubts, looking around as if she wants to suddenly disappear down a rabbit hole and pretend all this never

happened.

"Shayna, we have to be strong. Don't get weak now."

CHAPTER FORTY-ONE

THREE A.M. MOVES like a sloth when you're awake all night struggling for composure in nervous anticipation. Murray at last appears checking all along the walls and wiring as usual on his nightly rounds. Luckily no guards are in sight by the Gypsy barracks.

He nonchalantly unlocks and opens the electrical charge unit, follows a wire back about a foot, gnarls it up, then slightly puts small razor like cuts on it in several places. The red electrical light shorts out and goes off. Murray plants a rat's nest in and under the cut wires and nestles it in with a built-in conformity hiding it as a rat would do. He then closes and locks the charge box. Avoiding any suspicion, he then leaves in his usual relaxed manner going about his business toward the next barracks check.

The seven young Gypsies appear outside of their barracks like specters on the prowl. Pavel ambling lightly leans a step ladder against the electrical fence, climbs the ladder and cuts the three rows of barbwire fence with his wire cutters. The wires fall and Pavel pushes them aside. He grabs the top metal retaining pole and pulls himself up and with the utmost of caution climbs down the heavy vines growing on the other side of the fence.

Ivan is immediately behind him as he pulls himself up precisely with the accuracy of a lineman and climbs down the other side of the fence. The other Gypsies begin to follow suit up and down the ladder in a row of disappearance. The last Gypsy pulls himself up and readies to climb down the other side of the fence.

Being the final one over he seems to be feeling the blatant nervous tension waiting for him on the other side and their anxieties for him to hurry up appears to cut into his very soul. As his lips and hands tremble, he takes a deep breath giving the impression of pushing his nervous tension back into his very being. Fate is not with him tonight as he attempts to fastidiously scale the fence top. He accidently catches his shirt on a stray wire, loses his balance and falls to the ground. He makes a loud thud and a frazzled expulsion of air follows as he hits the ground.

Immediately the two Serbian guards in the watch towers on the fences respond with loud voices shouting in full chorus. "Attention! Attention! Prisoners escaping!"

The Serbian guard on the front corner shrieks the same again and begins shooting his rifle in controlled loud blasts near the area where the loud thud and scream originated. The second guard on the nearest side joins in firing his rifle into the same area, also without discrimination as to what or who he might be shooting.

Six dead young Gypsies lay on the ground in the dark outside of the camp near the cut fence. Their bullet riddled bodies are immediately surrounded by numerous armed guards holding bright military flashlights. Jingo swears and spits on the ground. "Bastard Gypsies, always causing trouble. Got me up in the middle of the night, for this? I otta piss on your dead bodies you pieces of shit."

The day light brings with it fear and distress as two male prisoners carry the Gypsy corpses from the outside of the fence to a small open military truck near the main courtyard gate. Their lifeless bodies are thrown into the back of it. They fall on top of each other with a *thud* that God seems to have forgotten. Murray watches from a distance and soundlessly blesses them, *God bless their souls.*

Two Serbian guards sit in the front seat of the truck. Jingo walks up in revulsion at the truck's deceased contents and waves his hand in good riddance as if shooing away flies. "Go bury these bastards! You know where."

CHAPTER FORTY-TWO

SEVERAL MEN STAND and gape at the repaired fence in the bright light of the next day wondering where to shift the blame and who will pay for this indiscretion. The electrical cage unit is open for inspection. Murray, German SS Officer Chief of Security Wilhelm Frolich, Commandant Willy Friedrich, Administrator Svetozar Vujkovic and Jingo stand near it. Officer Frolich checks the electrical cage unit as the others stand nearby.

The Commandant is the first to speak. "Security Chief Frolich, you will write a detailed report of your findings and present it tomorrow."

"Yes, Sir Commandant Friedrich." Frolich acknowledges and as his eyes pass Murray they lock with his ever so slightly and then abruptly unlock.

Administrator Vujkovic jumps in next. "What are your findings at this time Officer Frolich?" Security Officer Frolich continues with the inspection, checking the repaired wiring, "Murray, when was this unit repaired?"

"I repaired it immediately after the escaping prisoners were shot."

"Where is the damaged wire?"

Murray pulls the balled up wiring out of his pocket and hands it to Frolich. He turns the wire over several times in his hands and then smells it. He then inspects the cage unit smelling the wiring there. He then follows the wiring down about a foot and smells the new wiring. He then pulls a hidden rat's nest out from under the new wiring. "Here's your problem, rats. Rats chewed the wires and shorted out the unit." Officer Frolich stares at Murray.

"Yes sir," Murray holds back his anxiety.

Commandant Friedrich and Administrator Vujkovic stare at each other in wonder.

"Those damn Gypsies must stay up all night," Vujkovic frowns.

Commandant Friedrich narrows his eyes and shakes his head in consternation. "It doesn't make sense, something's missing."

"The bastards are dead!" Jingo blares out in defiance. "My guards killed them!"

The Commandant considers for a moment. "Roll call will be taken immediately in the Gypsy barracks to determine if any prisoners escaped."

"Yes, Sir Commandant," Jingo jumps to attention.

The following day barracks number ten is a hornet's nest of egos. Murray, Officer Frolich, Commandant Friedrich, Administrator Vujkovic and Jingo meet at an official table. Security Chief Frolich holds the finished official security documents pertaining to the Gypsy escape attempt as requested by Commandant Friedrich.

Officer Frolich stands at attention. "Commandant Friedrich, you will find this to be a detailed report, sir." Officer Frolich hands the Commandant the papers.

The Commandant takes them in hand. "Thank you Officer Frolich, you may sit now."

"Thank you sir," Frolich replies and sits back down at the table.

"What about the roll call?" The Commandant queries Jingo.

"Yes sir," Jingo stands up facing Commandant Friedrich. "It was determined that there were seven young Gypsies involved in the escape. Six were killed and one escaped."

"One escaped?" Vujkovic steams from his seat at the table. "Those bastard Gypsies all need to be sent to Auschwitz and sterilized."

The Commandant jeers at Vujkovic for his interruption. "That will be enough."

Vujkovic pulls back as if he inserted his foot in the wrong place, "Yes sir."

Jingo garners to himself climbing the ladder of power. That idiot can't keep his mouth shut which means more authority for me. I'll make the Commandant see that I'm the better man for the job. It's time to get rid of Vujkovic and make me the administrator of Banjica. Jingo snickers.

"And what is the name of the escapee?" The Commandant inquires.

Already standing, Jingo speaks the name with the utmost of command as if all inspection accolades lay with him, "Ivan Zeko."

Vujkovic jumps in again with unwarranted reactions to Jingo's rising star. "Ivan Zeko will be captured!"

The Commandant clears his throat, gives Vujkovic a look and continues. "Let it go for now. We can't spare the troops to find one freezing, starving Gypsy. He won't last long out there."

"Yes sir," Jingo and Vujkovic respond together like two kids rivaling for their dad's attention. The Commandant stands up first, then Vujkovic and Jingo, followed by Officer Frolich and then Murray.

"The camp will be cleared of all rats," The Commandant orders. "Is that clear Vujkovic?"

"Yes sir."

"All Gypsies will leave the camp as soon as possible." The Commandant demands. "There will be no more trouble."

"Yes sir," Jingo and Vujkovic respond together again, but Jingo isn't finished with Vujkovic yet. In his head Jingo realizes, Sometimes I feel on the verge of being buried alive by all this stress in my desires and hindered ambitions to be camp administrator. Damn that Vujkovic!

The Commandant leaves the table in pondering silence and trudges off toward his office as though he's thwarted by blithering idiots. Jingo and Vujkovic both looms basically coarse and uneducated. They defiantly glare at each other. Each is seemingly deep in their secret hopes of grasping an elusive promotion within the Regime. It is just beyond their reach, yet they continue to throw each other calculated mental threats. Both appear to comprehend the fact that their distance is never to be mediated or bridged and will remain snarling natural enemies for life.

CHAPTER FORTY-THREE

ONE INCIDENT AFFECTS the other and a deep, disturbing sorrow for some hangs over Banjica. While others' sorrows are a boon for the fascists, it comes as no surprise that justice and morality seem to have taken to the wind in the camp. Three-armed Serbian guards escort ten Gypsy women and girls dressed in camp uniforms across the main courtyard to a small waiting open truck.

Albert and Murray stand and watch. "Where are they taking them Murray?" Murray bunches up his face and looks away as if he isn't really there.

"Some of them are just young girls, only seven or eight years old." Albert distinctly objects.

"Well, I don't really know Albert." Murray stammers not wanting to face the obvious.

"Do you think? You know I've heard there are German run brothels in the larger camps."

"Probably Albert, I guess, probably so."

"Child molesters, they are all child molesters, scum of the earth."

Murray turns his head away again helpless and unable to rectify the situation.

"I can't watch this misery any longer. I'm embarrassed to be a human being. I'd rather be a rat. They treat each other with more respect." Albert swallows deep, blinking, and then turns back towards his barracks with the slow shuffle of a shattered soul.

The Gypsy women and girls get into the truck and it drives off into the distance.

A sign posted outside of the Gypsy barracks reads: ATTENTION:

All Gypsy Men, Women and Children will be transferred to the Semlin Sajmiste camp near Belgrade.

Five Serbian guards enter the Gypsy barracks. The Gypsies look up in wide-eyed fear as Jingo announces with his hand ready on his rifle. "All Gypsies will line up in the main courtyard at noon tomorrow, no exceptions, men, women and children!"

One Gypsy mother steps forward and pleads to Jingo. "Where are my baby girls? My twin girls are only seven years old. Where did you take my babies?"

Jingo approaches her and points his rifle at her head. "You will shut your mouth now!" The Gypsy mother falls to the floor weeping out of control.

Jingo momentarily contemplates pulling the trigger but then reconsiders, *Better not because the Commandant will be pissed off if these Gypsies riot. I must think about my promotion, but I'd love to kill this Gypsy bitch, maybe rape her first though. How dare she confront me... me, Jingo?*

Jingo lowers his rifle and orders his guards to back off and they all leave the barracks as the mother continues wailing on the floor.

CHAPTER FORTY-FOUR

THE GERMANS USE a mobile gas van for extermination at camps with no incinerators. The gas van waits in the main courtyard. About thirty Gypsies line up including, men, women and children. Armed Serbian guards surround them. Murray stands and watches.

Jingo smiles with the utmost of sincerity as he speaks to the Gypsies. "You will be transferred today to the Semlin Sajmiste Camp near Belgrade. It is a much better camp."

An older Gypsy man speaks out. "We don't want to go. We want to stay here or be released. We have done nothing to be imprisoned here in this death camp."

Jingo continues spreading confidence. "The other camp has larger barracks and cleaner living conditions. Some even have heat."

"You have heat here, but you let us Gypsies freeze. You lie. We have children with us." Jingo is becoming impatient, as if he had any to begin with. "All of you Gypsies will get into the van now!"

The older Gypsy man persists. "We will not get into the gas van!"

Jingo screams orders at Murray. "Murray, throw this blabbering old fool into the van!" Murray looks at Jingo as if he's crazy. "What? I will not! I'm an electrical engineer, not a kapo!" Murray is steadfast, nonverbally maintaining his employment status.

"Murray, that's an order!" Jingo shrieks losing his composure in the process. How dare you disobey my orders Murray, you will pay for this disrespect later, just wait. Jingo reflects to himself. I'll have you thrown in the gas van too. You're still a Jew.

Murray remains indignant and moves away like a raft floating above the storm. He appears unwilling to give into even one unforgiveable moral mistake that he may regret later in his lifetime. A second older Gypsy man berates Jingo and his gaggle of guards. "You're all Serbs and Slavs and you kill your own people, the poor peasant farmers so the Germans can steal their land. You are all trash! Human garbage! Blithering idiots to Hitler, a madman destined to destroy himself with his own hatred. Whatever you put out into the ether eventually comes back to you!"

Jingo appears to regain his composure, but a foul scowl adamantly crosses his face. "We do what the Germans tell us to do!"

The second older Gypsy man forewarns with passion. "You deserve to die for that!"

The first Serbian guard comes over and points a rifle at the old Gypsy man, but he is unafraid in the face of death. He seems to know that 'it will have him today one way or the other' just like his obvious camp weariness and its complete and utter consumption of him.

Jingo shrieks again to the second older Gypsy. "Get into the van, now!"

The old Gypsy forewarns. "You will die today Jingo along with me. I have seen your death. It has finally returned to you."

"What?" For a fleeting moment Jingo glowers into the eyes of the old Gypsy floating into the ether of a speechless face. He lets the prediction sink in briefly as the startling perceptive power emanating from the old Gypsy suddenly gives the man a superior focal point as ominous as distant gunshots.

Abruptly changing personalities again, Jingo impulsively falls back infuriated, catching himself in disbelief and not willing to give his power away to the old Gypsy, nor change his allegiances unless there is money involved. He glares in horror at the Gypsy and then motions an order of death to the waiting old man who continues staring at Jingo. It's like he's an ethereal spirit or maybe even a ghoul, Jingo thinks to himself as though the old man is waiting, unmoved for the inevitable.

The first Serbian guard shoots the second older Gypsy in the head and he falls to the ground dead. The Gypsy women grab their young boys and back off, seeming to hide nowhere but everywhere in the open. Jingo stares for a moment at the boys and blindly rationalizes to himself. What a shame to kill these beautiful young morsels of desire, he pushes back his lust. Too bad not even one of these pussy guards wants to admit that they would like to be alone with the young Gypsy boys. Such a delight they would be. Jingo lingers in silence with himself, his fantasy libido thrusting out in his front zipper. If there was only a way to get these young boys away from their parents, let me think now.

The first older Gypsy man shrieks at Jingo, waking him from his pedophile fantasy. "You bastard hypocrites!" The old Gypsy then physically attacks the first Serbian guard. There is a loud brawl. One of the other guards shoots the old Gypsy and he falls to the ground dead.

The other older Gypsy men physically assault all the Serbian guards. Attending sudden death screeches and indiscriminate rifle fire fills the ruthless madness and turmoil of the main courtyard.

In a savage burst Jingo cries out, holding his chest as he stumbles, falling to the ground. All the older Gypsy men lay dead on the ground as well. Two Serbian guards have been critically wounded and hobble away with blood trailing behind them. The Gypsy women and their young boys start to weep, suddenly realizing their hapless fate without their men to protect them.

As Jingo lies on the ground, he tries to turn his head and beg for help, but his body will not move, and his mouth will not open. What's happening to me, have I been shot? Jingo muses to himself. I hear the guards above me milling around and mumbling to each other, but I can't really understand them because they seem so far away. Jingo tries to perk his ears, but to no avail. Are they taking me to the infirmary? Please help me Lord, I don't want to die, he reminisces in his head. No, no, I can't die now because I'm going to be Administrator of Banjica soon. A silent sob engulfs him. God, please help me. Jingo feels that he is being lifted somewhere. Yes, I'm going to the hospital now, he remembers the hospital as his blood flows away. Abruptly Jingo is slammed onto a truck. What? Where am I going? Why are they dumping me onto a truck so hard? Jingo listens to his mind. I am a patient and should be treated kindly. Jingo hears the words now, Belgrade Firing Range somewhere in a cloud of haze. No! No! You can't throw me into the death pit with the Gypsies. No! No! I am Jingo. I am somebody! I am somebody!

The surviving guards threaten the Gypsy women and boys with rifles and the women get into the gas van. The children beg and fall to the ground. The guards pick them up and throw them headfirst into the van as if they were sacks of garbage and they hit the floor with a thud. The children's tears start, but the guards ignore it and seal the door to the gas van shut and then lock it behind them.

Two German guards drive the gas van as it follows a small car driven by Administrator Vujkovic to the firing ranges on the outskirts of Belgrade. Now I'm in total control without that loser Jingo in my hair, Vujkovic smiles to himself with a smirk as he remembers his arguments, differences and putdowns by Jingo. Good riddance you bastard.

Once the gas van nears the Belgrade firing ranges, one of the German guards stops the van, exits the truck, and crawls underneath it, diverting its exhaust into the interior of the van. The Gypsy prisoners inside scream and bang on the gas van's door as they die of carbon monoxide gas poisoning. There is an endless roar, too terrible to be heard.

The German guard gets back into the truck and indifferently drives on. The two German guards share a cigarette and joke about the dying Gypsies as they go.

Once the van enters the firing ranges on the outskirts of Belgrade ten male inmates appear like ghouls to dig mass graves. The rear of the van tilts over a mass grave and the door of the van opens. With the help of the German guards, the asphyxiated corpses are dumped into the freshly dug holes. Another small truck follows carrying the dead corpses of the older gypsy males. The gravediggers jump onto the truck and throw these dead bodies into the mass graves as well.

Jingo's body lies alone on the open military truck. Administrator Vujkovic stands and looks down at Jingo's corpse. A bloody rifle wound penetrates his heart. Vujkovic orders all guards and gravediggers to leave him alone with Jingo so that he can pay his last funeral rites to the dead man. Everyone leaves and Vujkovic is alone with Jingo's body. You lowlife scum, Vujkovic flares, red faced to himself. You caused me so much frustration and anxiety challenging me all the time and reporting me to the Commandant like a grade school kid, you piece of shit.

"What?" Vujkovic stares down at Jingo's two tone black and white shoes, the very ones that Jingo pilfered from Vujkovic in the baggage storage room. "Gimme back my shoes, you prick." Vujkovic reaches down and rips the shoes off of Jingo and throws them aside on the truck.

Jingo's eyes are closed, but he somehow senses Vujkovic above him and tries to wiggle a little finger for help. Barely conscious Jingo mutters in his head. Death is trying to take me, I feel claustrophobic, suffocated and so helpless with this sharp pain in my chest, and now... now I feel dullness. I was a good man. I don't deserve to die like this. I'm an important man, not some Gypsy trash to be thrown down into a death pit still alive. Terrified by the breakdown of his body, Jingo doesn't go easily into dying. Just like in life, inadequacies flood him, even in death.

Vujkovic spits on Jingo's face and then looks up to see if anyone is watching, I gotta be careful Vujkovic's mind rationalizes and then begins again. What the hell is your real name anyway, did you ever really know? Jingo, that's an idiot's name. I'd piss on your body, but I might be seen, or someone might smell my urine and the Commandant wouldn't like such disrespect of one of our own, Vujkovic mulls silently to himself not wanting to draw attention.

Vujkovic then motions to the guards that he has finished the funeral rites for one Jingo, Penniless piece of shit, uneducated, drunken, whoremonger, part-time child molester and family deserter, Vujkovic guffaws to himself. I'd break your legs and put you in the hospital, but you're already dead.

Vujkovic then gives his Serbian guards orders to throw Jingo's presumed dead body into the same pit with the Gypsy corpses. Ashes to ashes, dust to dust you miserable bastard, Vujkovic thinks briefly, and smirks again to himself.

CHAPTER FORTY-FIVE

ALBERT SITS BEHIND the prisoner's barracks at noon eating his lunch and freeing himself temporarily from his stifling, miserable banker's job. The warm spring air floats with him into the sights and smells of new life with a temporary merge of happiness in the natural world. Wildflowers poke their head up in defiance of the harsh winter as buzzing bees circle them, busy collecting the valuable pollen for their queen.

Albert scans the horizon and abruptly spies a woman that looks like Shayna. He closes his eyes trying to drive out the thought since Shayna look-a-likes constantly haunt him. He's always imagining that he sees her face in the small groups of women who are lucky enough to be left alive in Banjica.

The look-a-like stands oblivious behind the locked chain-link fence with her face up in the warm sunshine. She wears a colorful peasant dress with a simple scarf covering her hair.

Albert waves and calls to her, "Hello, hello."

The woman looks up at Albert and a startled expression passes over her face as she struggles with mixed emotions. Fear, horror, delight and then shock all seem to appear then disappear.

"Shayna, Shayna, is that you?" Albert cries almost begging in a harsh desperation, his entire being suddenly lined with pain and hardship.

The woman stares back at Albert and momentarily considers responding and waving back, but then she stops herself abruptly and reconsiders.

Albert is screaming now. "Shayna, come to the gate! I miss you!"

The woman pulls her scarf down over her face and hesitates

again as what to do next.

"Hello, Shayna, hello," Albert jumps up and down swiftly shifting gears, smiling and waving now like a happy child.

The woman puts her hand to her face in a weeping gesture and then turns and cautiously ambles back toward the small cottages surrounding the larger house. Albert stares on in silent heartbreak adding to his personal array of hatred, darkness, despair and finally disappointment as he holds back the stabbing pressure of tears.

Five months pregnant Shayna stands to the far-right side of Administrator Vujkovic in the main courtyard. A firing squad of five Serbian guards stands in front of Shayna with their rifles raised and pointed at her. Shayna trembles and holds her pregnant stomach.

"Ready, aim..." Vujkovic yells orders to his guards.

Unexpectedly Albert appears and stands in front of Shayna. "I did it! She had nothing to do with stealing the diamonds! Stop! It was my idea! Stop... now!" Albert orders in a heaving frenzy.

Shayna jumps up from her bed in terror, fiercely shaking and trembling. Wilhelm wakes up startled, rubs his head, moans and jumps up still half asleep.

"What is it? What's wrong?" Wilhelm demands of Shayna's quivering tears.

Shayna holds her pregnant stomach as her voice breaks. "My baby, my baby, they're going to shoot my baby. They're going to kill us both." She speaks with haste near shouting which instantly throws a rush of panic into Wilhelm as well.

"What?" Officer Wilhelm Frolich is as blanched as the white sheet that he sleeps on. Like the devastating shock of a dream, the shutters of the house rattle in the wind.

Albert and Murray are alone in their cell.

"I think that I saw Shayna today." Albert smiles in a dubious happiness.

"What?"

"Yea, Shayna, but the woman looked heavier than Shayna, you know, fatter."

"Where?"

"There's a house in back of all the barracks. A locked chain-link fence separates them." Murray's eyes freeze in heavy trepidation as he holds a glare of annoyance on Albert.

"Look son, you just can't go there." Murray attempts the family bond.

"What?" Albert attempts to suppress his newfound obsession.

"Please just stay away from that house. You could get us all killed by snooping around there."

Without a movement, Albert's lips slightly part into the draw of a smile. "But, she's my wife."

"Albert, please. You must forget about Shayna for now. When the war is over, then you can see her again."

"What war is that?" Albert's lips now twist into an odd painful beam of a distorted grin.

Murray frowns at Albert in perplexed alarm. "What did you just say? Was that a joke?"

Albert folds away and a blank stare crosses his face, "Nothing, ah, about what?"

"Did you just ask me, what war?"

"Ah well, did I? I guess so, I don't know, ha, ha." Albert shines a mixture of awe and amusement. Murray pulls away in deep sorrow and immediate worry.

CHAPTER FORTY-SIX

AT THREE IN the morning Albert stands alone at the gate to the house in back of the prisoner's barracks. Shayna and Officer Frolich are in bed asleep. There is a soft knock on their bedroom door. Wilhelm gets up and answers it. It's Mimi.

"Sir, sorry to bother you this time of night, but there is someone at the gate."

Wilhelm swallows hard and rubs his eyes. "What time is it?"

"Three a.m.," Mimi whispers disconcerted but firm.

"Okay, Mimi, I'll be right down, thank you." Mimi leaves. Wilhelm puts on his clothes. Shayna wakes up, "What's going on?"

"You stay here. I'm going down to see who's at the gate."

"What, the gate?"

Nodding his head in affirmation, Wilhelm leaves the bedroom. Shayna pulls herself up from the bed. She is five months pregnant and it shows. Waddling to the bedroom window, she looks out. A vague figure stands behind the gate, almost phantom like in the foggy night air.

Mimi moves to the locked gate in a suppressed dread as the spring wind swirls around the house and vibrates the gate. Albert stands there with a stone face as hard as the cement walk on which he stands. *Oh my God,* she hesitates in thought. *What can this crazy man want at this time in the morning?*

"What is it, sir?" Mimi demands straight away.

"I'm looking for my wife Shayna. Is she here?"

Mimi stares at Albert as if he's deranged. "I don't know who that is, so please just go away before the guard on the gate tower above us sees you. You may be shot at any moment."

Albert disregards her request in blissful ignorance, just like his mother and her rose colored glasses. He remains adamant in his delirious obsession. "I want to speak to my wife Shayna."

Mimi's mouth turns down with a mixture of fear and loathing at the demanding consumed man standing in front of her. She ponders the consequences momentarily. *This annoying man could get us all killed at any moment.* Mimi glances up at the guard tower above her and all is silent.

"Just a moment then," Mimi has to give in or wake the guard. She turns around with a controlled swiftness of direction and marches carefully back into the house without a sound.

Shayna gives it her best pace out of the house, down the walk way and up to the locked gate. Albert gapes at her in complete and total shock.

"Shayna, Shayna," Albert lets loose at the mercy of Shayna's tears. "You're pregnant!" He suddenly locks his voice in cruel judgment.

Shayna shoots Albert a sharp look of abject fright knowing the danger overhead and wipes her glistening eyes, "Albert, why did you come here?"

"What? To see you Shayna," a little boy emerges now sorry that he passed judgment on her. Shayna glares at Albert for just a few seconds too long instinctively familiar with the feeling and knowing that something is not quit right with him.

Oh my God, she senses, *Albert is losing his mind. He's reached the end of his rope.* Shayna points up to the guard post above them. "If you wake him up, we could all be shot because of you. Why are you putting us in this danger?"

The little boy starts to tear. "I just had to see you. I have no one else to talk to. Everyone in my family is either gone or dead."

Shayna relents a bit but seems to sense that she must keep this conversation under her control. "Oh Albert, I'm so sorry that it turned out this way, but there is nothing that I can do right now."

"Why are you pregnant?" Albert asks this time with an unruffled inquiry.

"I was kidnapped, but now I'm alright, and I'm in no danger,

Albert, unless you put me in danger and get me killed."

"But you are my wife," the controlled tranquility still there.

Shayna holds back. If little boy Albert's throws a tantrum, she surmises, then there will be trouble because he's now becoming a burden to bear rather than a shock at the gate.

Albert instinctively senses he's becoming more of an annoyance than husband and falls into childlike giggling. It's a distraction revealing his sense of hopelessness, and he pouts like a baby.

An expression of pain suddenly takes over Shayna's being as she trips and falls into Albert's emotional pit of hot and cold. "I don't know why this all is happening to us Albert. Fate I guess, but please believe me, I will see you after the war. I promise you this with all my heart."

Albert fumbles a long instant as if he's regaining control over his digressive erratic emotions. However, dribs and drabs of occasional words mumble and tumble out of his mouth, giving him away.

"Albert, I still love you, I do, but we are all prisoners. So please, I beg of you, just go now."

Albert appears to sense a familiar rage building up inside of him giving off a deep scowl like a terrible smoldering ember. With a sudden affliction of presumed neglect and then seemingly remembered bitterness, Albert's mood shockingly swings into a frantic reversal. Within an instant the madman reappears with a hideous jealous vengeance. "No! You are my wife and you are coming with me! Now!"

Shayna gapes at Albert again in a terrifying dread and plants both of her hands over her face as if to disappear from all the insanity.

"Do you hear me?" Albert screams through the locked fence. "Have them open this gate now!" Albert grabs the chain-link fence and starts to shake and rattle it like he's locked inside an insane asylum.

The watch tower guard slithers down from his post and stands directly behind Albert who, in his badgering rant, doesn't even notice him.

Albert shrieks again. "Open this gate, now!"

Seeing no other way around Albert the Banker's consuming rage, the watch tower guard hits him over the head with his rifle butt. Albert groans in agony and falls to the ground in a forlorn heap.

CHAPTER FORTY-SEVEN

ALBERT AND MURRAY sit together alone in their cell. Albert has an ice pack held to his head with bandages. "My head feels like a water balloon."

"Why did you do such a stupid thing? I told you not to go there!"

"I just couldn't help myself. I can't really remember a lot of things anymore."

"You could have gotten Shayna killed!" Murray states the obvious not wanting any excuses.

"I know, but I saw her. I saw Shayna and she's pregnant with someone else's baby."

Murray narrows his eyes and looks away in a silent, agitated but mature contemplation as if finally knowing that he has to accept human nature now.

"Let's go rescue her!" Albert lets it fly out.

"And bring her to where? To this dangerous dump so that she can face the firing squad, pregnant? You talk like a silly little kid."

"The firing squad? What for?"

"Jingo convinced Vujkovic that she talked you into stealing diamonds."

"What? That was my idea, besides Jingo's dead."

"Jingo may be dead, and thank God for that, but his evil still lingers on."

"But, why blame Shayna?"

"Albert, the woman will always take the blame. War is a man's game."

"But I just wanted to escape this prison and be with my wife."

"You're thinking of you and your needs, not hers. You're still a selfish little boy!"

The room fills with an awkward silence as if the blunt truth may finally start to sink into Albert's head.

"She is okay, right?" Murray lays out his concern.

Albert yet appears unconvinced. "Yea," he stammers, "but I..."

Murray's voice rises to a horrendous squawk. "There is no but! You will get her killed! You will get me killed. The Germans will probably torture you to death for being an idiot! Do you think that these hard core, sadistic killers give a shit about your girlfriend and how much you care? Quit being a stupid kid!"

"Okay, okay I'm sorry," Albert pulls away as though he is finally thumped on the head.

"You must never, ever go there again! You're lucky that you're the banker and that you make them laugh or you would be dead right now!"

"Okay, alright."

"Albert, adulthood isn't a must. It's a choice, so make that choice and face it!"

Albert agrees with a harsh nod groaning in pain as he rubs his head with the ice pack.

"I'm so sorry that your family is dead, and I know that you're still in emotional shock, but you must find a way to regain your self-control."

Albert nods, "Yes sir."

"Keep the ice on your head or you will have a blood clot."

Murray checks an open electrical unit in front of barracks five. Sad memories of the Gypsies and their tragedies swarm back into his head, but he drives them out thinking, *I can't dwell on how unjust and severe life is here in Banjica, or I will end up just like Albert, detached from reality.* Murray is drawn back in regardless. *What horrible human sorrows will we have to endure next? What repulsive criminals wait for us and to do what to us?* Murray puts his hand to his forehead and physically tries to force out the melancholy before it walks freely in his head like a garden where nothing grows.

Interrupting Murray's self-analysis, Officer Frolich shows up and begins inspecting the same electrical unit. Murray looks over at him and mutters to himself throwing it off. They are alone and talk freely.

"If Albert comes to the gate again, I must have him shot immediately for trespassing." Frolich means business.

"I already told him that, but I'll do it again." Murray shakes a mean nod.

"Does he understand, or has he lost his mind? Is he crazy?"

Murray drops his eyes. "He is, yes, losing his mind."

"If he tells anyone anything, I will deny it all and he will be executed for false accusations."

"I will tell him that too."

"Does he know who lives with Shayna?"

"No, he does not." Murray is sure of this.

"Then keep it that way, okay?" There is no friendship left in Frolich.

"Yes, yes I certainly will! You can count on that!"

Murray closes up the electrical unit and Officer Frolich walks away and nonchalantly inspects another electrical unit further down the line.

Murray ambles into their barracks and finds Albert lying on his bed staring up at the ceiling, lost in a vacant gaze. They are alone. Murray sits down on the side of Albert's bed holding onto a somber, cold grimace.

"Are you awake, Albert?"

''I'm depressed."

"This is very important Albert, are you listening?"

"Yes sir."

"There are now orders to execute you on sight if you trespass at the back house again. Do you understand the gravity of this order?"

"Yes sir, I do."

"You will not talk about what happened or what you saw at the house to anyone. This is a life or death matter for every one of us Albert. Do you get it?"

"Yes sir, I understand."

"I can't help you anymore Albert, it is beyond my reach."

"Yes sir, I understand perfectly."

Murray aims a cold, hard determined shot into Albert's eyes, then gets up and leaves.

Albert works at his desk as banker in barracks number ten. He appears worn, tired and dejected. Impulsively Albert jumps up, rips off his head bandage and flings it onto the floor. Slamming himself back into his seat, Albert holds his head down and weeps bitterly to himself.

Stjepan Filipovic is a twenty-five-year-old Croatian partisan who reached the status of Yugoslav Resistance Commander at an early age because of his loyalty, military daring, astute intelligence and his formal military relationship with Yugoslav Field Commander Josip Broz Tito.

Filipovic is Commander in Valjevo, Serbia by 1941 and continually implores the people to never stop fighting for their freedom from the evils of fascism. His intense charisma, strength and humanity for the common man are undeniable. For this and more he is singled out and targeted for his superior leadership abilities. Possibly blinded by his own youthful exuberance, this oversight may have led Filipovic to be captured on February 24, 1942 by Axis forces and scheduled to be hanged on May 22, 1942.

In Valjevo, four-armed Serbian guards lead Stjepan Filipovic up to a noose to face an early death as a Communist war resister. As the rope is put around his neck, Filipovic holds fast to his beliefs even in the face of his demise. He rebelliously lifts his unfettered arms and clenched fists up to eternity and the everlasting as he screams for the entire gathered crowd to hear: "Smrt fasizmu, sloboda narodu!" which translates as, 'Death to fascism, freedom to the people!' Stjepan embodies his reason for living as he goes to his death for freedom.

Stjepan Filipovic is declared a National Hero of Yugoslavia on

December 14, 1949 and a statue of him stands in the town of Valjevo cast after the very photo snapped the minute of his defiant yell. It becomes the war cry of the very partisans who will lead the Balkans to a crucial victory.

About six months after Nurse Judith leaves without a trace, a letter from the local police department arrives demanding that Mr. and Mrs. Frolich appear before the Circuit Court Judge for child support. The letter also reads that a Wilhelm Frolich, seventeen, had impregnated a Judith Helgar, Practical Nurse while working in the Frolich household for a named three months and that Wilhelm's family would be responsible for child support for eighteen years.

Wilhelm's parents are fuming with anger both at Nurse Judith for molesting an underage boy and at their own randy son. Wilhelm stands by his allegations that he is innocent and never had full on sex with the nurse, but only engaged in heavy petting. Wilhelm is drug into court several more times and the last time being when Nurse Judith stands holding her newborn baby.

"I didn't do it!" Irritation slips into Wilhelm's voice as he tries to lower his tone in spite of Nurse Judith crying and holding her baby lovingly in her blest arms as hurt fills her face. Wilhelm's words register with her, but she keeps a stern, cold upper lip as she takes a quick swipe of her misty eyes with the back of her hand casting a long drawn out look at Wilhelm as if saying, 'How dare you question me'.

The entire story is published in the legal section of the local newspaper and everyone in Wilhelm's high school catches an earful of the tasty, juicy story. When Wilhelm goes to class no one will talk to him except his crippled neighbor Bruno, who wants to know 'where he can find a nurse like Judith.' The principal calls Wilhelm into his office again and tells him that the school is considering not letting him attend senior graduation in the spring, but the school board will vote on it. When Wilhelm walks down the hall, he hears the word *pervert* yelled at him at every turn. Trying to ignore the cutting jabs and wearing a distant distracted look, Wilhelm often feels just like another shadow among the shadows.

At long last when the baby is four months old the true father, a twenty-five-year-old, comes forward saying that he finally found a good paying job and that he and Judith could now get married and take care of their baby themselves. Despite the fact that Mr. Frolich is bristling at the lie, and Wilhelm's parents are given the opportunity to prosecute both Judith and her future, irresponsible husband for perjury and general menace, ultimately, they relent and in the end are happy just to have Wilhelm's name cleared. Finding the baby's rightful parents combined with life being back to normal again and a married sixty-year-old, slightly overweight lady with four grandchildren now acting as Grandma's nurse, confines Wilhelm mostly to his room now.

CHAPTER FORTY-EIGHT

SHAYNA AND WILHELM sit and each lunch in the dining room area. Mimi enters and hands Wilhelm a sealed letter. He opens it, reading silently to himself. A scowl of dread crosses his face.

"What is it Wilhelm?"

"It's from the Commandant. He's requesting a meeting with me."

Shayna stares in worry, "about what?"

"The letter doesn't say."

Their eyes meet in nervous tension.

Officer Frolich waits outside of German Commandant Willie Friedrich's closed office door. Mumbles of dull cut-off conversations seep out under the door and seem to pour out whiffs of foul odors into his nostrils like the boiling refuse from a rendering plant. *God help me, I hate this place*, Frolich mulls reflecting on the horrors of the recent past.

An antique wall clock beats out the seconds as Frolich's eyes linger with every tick between compulsive intervals and nervous glances at the Commandant's closed office door. *How did I get myself into this?* Frolich deliberates to himself. *This is way too much tension and stress for me, but I must think about our baby. Yes, I'm going to be a father soon.*

Finally, the office door opens and Administrator Vujkovic appears dressed in official military attire. "You may come in now Officer Frolich." Frolich stands up and formally walks into the Commandant's office. Commandant Friedrich sits at an official table and is immediately joined by Vujkovic.

"Please have a seat Officer Frolich." The Commandant motions for Frolich to sit down. Frolich takes a quick glance around the office. A large picture of Adolf Hitler peers down menacingly from behind the Commandant's desk, like the eyes of God watching all. Frolich briefly lingers on the snapshot of Hitler in his omnipresence and gives up a slight bit of nausea but then pushes it back down and sits.

"So, Officer Frolich," Commandant Friedrich entertains. "How are you?"

"Fine today, thank you Herr Commandant." Officer Frolich forces it out.

"Oh Vujkovic, get Officer Frolich a drink, will you?"

Vujkovic stands up at attention and then addresses Officer Frolich. "What is your pleasure?"

"Oh, no thank you sir." Officer Frolich appreciates with a smile. "I'm fine."

Vujkovic nods formally and sits back down at the official table.

"So, Officer Frolich," Commandant Friedrich continues. "We may have a problem here."

Officer Frolich glances up in question thinking to himself, *Oh my God, I feel like I'm going to vomit on this table.*

Administrator Vujkovic looks over at Frolich. "Are you okay Officer Frolich?"

"Yes sir, I'm fine Administrator Vujkovic." Officer Frolich pulls it together and swallows. "Just a little indigestion from breakfast this morning," Frolich settles it.

Commandant Friedrich has his say. "Yes, the food here is less than desirable, I agree."

The Commandant snickers. Vujkovic laughs out loud.

The Commandant resumes. "Officer Frolich, in my duty as Commandant for the Regime, I've been called upon to help organize, shall we say, the inmates at the Jasenovac Camp in Croatia."

"Yes sir." Relaxing his stomach, Officer Frolich responds staring dead on at the Commandant.

"I will be gone for a week and I wanted to make sure that you stayed here at all times in barracks ten until my return."

Officer Frolich accepts in a formal acquiesce of acknowledgement.

"You will be helping out Murray Weinberg, and you both will be on extreme alert."

Officer Frolich swallows releasing some tension. "Yes sir, absolutely. I will do that."

Commandant Friedrich concurs in compliance and self-satisfaction, "fine then, fine."

There is an uneasy quiet as if the meeting is officially over but something more is to come. "Will that be all sir?" Officer Frolich signals in respect and acceptance.

"Yes, for now Officer Frolich." The Commandant returns the affirmation.

Officer Frolich then stands up, salutes Commandant Friedrich in formal Nazi style, turns and walks toward the door.

"Oh yes, Officer Frolich," Commandant Friedrich speaks to Frolich's back.

Frolich hears the words that abruptly stop his quick escape, *Oh God, here it comes.* Silence hangs like a cloud in the room for seconds that seems like hours to Frolich as his restored churning stomach lets out a low growl. He turns around falling to attention once more and yet again faces the Commandant at the mercy of his aching body and simultaneously wishing for unspoken mercy, *God bless our child.*

"Just a word of advice from someone a little older than you Officer Frolich," The Commandant gloats all knowing.

Officer Frolich stares at Commandant Friedrich in an affected, relaxed question. "Yes sir?"

"Don't get so involved with one woman and especially if nothing can become of it." Officer Frolich narrows his eyes in understanding and continues with his respectful attention. "Back off for a while and visit the brothels when I get back, you know, give yourself some distance." The Commandant suggests with a wry smirk as if Frolich really doesn't know what he's missing. Administrator Vujkovic lets out a worldly chuckle as though he holds the ultimate and proud record in brothel indiscretions.

"Yes, Commandant Friedrich," Officer Frolich remarks in a for-

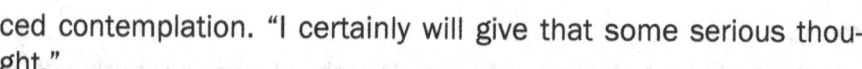

ced contemplation. "I certainly will give that some serious thought."

The Commandant smiles like a sly fox. "Shall we say, give yourself an escape route. Women can trap you, especially when they know there is no future with them."

Officer Frolich smiles back and nods his head in complete thanks at both the Commandant and Vujkovic as if he really cares about their suggestions. "Yes, sir and thank you both for the valuable advice, I certainly will take heed."

Shayna and Officer Wilhelm Frolich sit on the sofa in their living quarters. "You must learn German; I will teach you."

"I already know a little of the language," Shayna replies.

"You must be fluent. It might save our lives someday and we must think of our baby too."

Shayna smiles and holds her stomach. "Well, okay then teach me Wilhelm."

"Good, we'll start tonight."

Shayna and Officer Frolich sit at a table with paper and pencils in front of them. "Okay, Shayna, first you will speak the sentence and then you will write it down."

"Okay then Wilhelm, go ahead."

"Wir reisen mach Deutschland Landshut," Frolich speaks slowly. 'We're traveling to Landshut, Germany." Now repeat that in German, Shayna."

"Wir reisen mach Deutschland Lanshut," Shayna repeats it slowly trying her best for the accurate accent.

"Okay, now write it down." Frolich hands her the paper and pencil. Shayna takes them and starts writing.

CHAPTER FORTY-NINE

BELLA HARVESTS VEGETABLES from a garden behind the house which she and Walter planted earlier in the spring. As Bella attends to the garden, Walter rakes leaves and other debris off of the weedy self-planted grass and walk area. Mimi walks out and gives them both a glass of ice water and a light snack.

A large, dark cloud of smoke floats by overhead, not unnoticed by the three of them. Walter runs to his mother in fear as he points up to the sky. "What's that Mom, it smells funny?" Bella stops her gardening abruptly and looks up, *gun power,* she surmises with a startle.

Bella shoots Mimi a frantic stare and Mimi lifts her shoulders up into a question mark. "I don't know Bella. I've never seen anything like it before." Bella tries to hold back her anxiety as Walter closes in on her for a hug.

The hum is like a mosquito at first, a thin high-pitched reverberation. As they perk their ears, a distant buzz like a swarm of wasps is rapidly approaching them in the distance somewhere.

"What's that noise?" Walter's jaw hinges as he glares around looking for the source of the clatter. He shoots his eyes up to the distant sky as the sound grows louder, then becomes a roar as the military planes approach them. "It's coming from the sky." Walter points up and shouts.

Bella jerks her body to attention expecting the worst as the roar intensifies and draws upon them. "Get into the bungalows, now!" she screams at Walter.

Suddenly the planes are right above them with deafening engine blasts that send them scurrying toward their bungalows. A rush of wind starts and then turns into a mountain of power that throws Walter to the ground. "Get up now Walter!" Bella runs toward Walter and drags him toward the bungalows. Mimi rushes to help her. Bella glances back before she shuts the bungalow door and the planes are so low that they almost seem to be crashing into Banjica.

As Wilhelm sits in his senior history class, thoughts of his recently deceased grandmother invade his head. As a boy, she took care of him while both his parents were at work. He always seemed to be her favorite grandchild. He did have several cousins, but Wilhelm was always the one to receive the most favors and gifts from Grandma. While the other grandchildren would appear not to notice, Wilhelm is sure that they secretly resented him for getting most of her attention. Sometimes his cousins would pull mean tricks on him out of jealousy, but he would never tell his grandmother on them fearing meaner tricks to come.

One week has passed since her funeral, but the shock of her sudden death still haunts Wilhelm. He is now seventeen and getting ready to graduate from high school. He still misses and treasures Grandma more than any other relative including his parents who, apart from the chess games, were mostly missing during his childhood. His father, a university professor, and his mother, a high school teacher, are to this day mostly involved in their separate careers. This is just as they were during his childhood development giving it up to Grandma who despite her loving nature was a religious prude. According to Wilhelm, she was a fanatic that thought talking about the birds and the bees was a sin. She was the mother of three healthy children including Wilhelm's mother. Even so, she was always adamant about telling Wilhelm that she and her husband only engaged in sexual relations for reproductive purposes. She believed unyieldingly in her resolve that any carnal urges were against God's will. Wilhelm often remembers long after Grandma's husband is gone that, *Maybe this is why Grandpa was always so mean. He was a sexually frustrated man who probably thought that secretly relieving himself would send him to Hell.*

Trying to hold back his tears in class, Wilhelm puts his head down pretending to be sick and feigned a headache. *I don't want anyone, especially these boys to see me cry,* but he feels so sad and disconnected.

"Are you okay?" Wilhelm's teacher asks, but he would not raise his head. As the tears pour out onto his desk, the teacher suggests that Wilhelm go to the school nurse.

"No, no," Wilhelm's mumbles squeak out from under his folded arms and he manages to shake his head in the negative. The boys in the class began to snicker at each other and laugh at Wilhelm, somehow sensing that it's a lie and a cover-up.

The teacher lets Wilhelm alone and when the class bell rings, the other students stand up and leave the classroom. Wilhelm finally raises his head and his red swollen eyes drip with tears.

"What's wrong?" Wilhelm's teacher begs to help him.

Wiping his tears Wilhelm murmurs, it out. "My grandmother just died and I'm still in shock...I guess. She died so suddenly that I didn't even have a chance to say goodbye and apologize for my bad behavior."

"I'm so very sorry Wilhelm," his teacher comforts him.

"Thank you, Mrs. Helmuth."

"If you need to talk about it, please feel free to consult with me anytime, okay Wilhelm?"

"Okay," Wilhelm confides as he stands up, smiles back at her and leaves the room dragging his feet.

Outside in the hallway the boys in his history class are waiting for him and randomly laugh, imitating him crying. "Oh boo-who, boo-who, you queer... ha... ha... ha!"

Infuriated, Wilhelm starts screaming at them. "What is it now? Am I a queer or a pervert?"

The team captain shouts back. "Both!"

CHAPTER FIFTY

SHAYNA AND OFFICER Frolich eat lunch. Their two-year-old son, Thomas, sits with them Still in a highchair. Mimi brings a letter and hands it to Officer Frolich. "Thank you, Mimi." Mimi nods and then leaves. Frolich opens it immediately and reads silently to himself.

"What is it Wilhelm?"

"It's from my mother in Germany. She tells me that my father is dying from his weak heart."

"I'm so sorry Wilhelm."

"Thank you love," Wilhelm reaches over, and kisses Shayna then kisses their son.

Little Thomas laughs, swings his arms in the air and smiles, feeling loved.

"We will all three go to my parent's house in Landshut, Germany."

Shayna gazes hesitantly at Wilhelm.

"You and little Thomas will stay there in secret until the war is over."

"Well, I just can't desert my mother and brother here alone."

"Your father, Murray, will take care of them."

Shayna shifts uneasily in her chair.

"I will give him access to the house as a security measure." Shayna's uneasiness turns into a nervous facial question.

"The war is coming to an end Shayna. In February of forty-three the Soviet Army drove Germany out of Russia and the British Army drove Germany out of Italy and France too." Shayna pulls back in astonishment; she has no radio or any other news source available to her. "In April of forty-four the Allies and Tito's Yugoslav Partisans dropped bombs on the Semlin Sajmiste Camp on the outskirts of Belgrade, and amazingly Romania and the other Balkan countries just withdrew from the Axis forces and have now joined the Allies." Shayna flinches in angry tension at being kept in the dark about the latest war news. "Germany is losing the war."

Shayna pulls her lips into a half smile. "So, the Germans will be gone soon?"

Officer Frolich nods affirmatively. "I do love my beautiful Germany, but not their bloody, blasted war. Hitler's a madman. Germany is in ruins again because of him, the Allied forces have bombed the hell out of Germany."

"But Wilhelm, won't they try and capture you now?"

"Yes love, they will, and you must prepare yourself for it."

Shayna pulls away in reaction and picks up young Thomas.

"I didn't participate in any of the killings or tortures like the guards, and there is no proof that I committed any crimes against humanity; I'm just a conscripted soldier that was forced into a duty or death situation by my country of birth."

Shayna nods in acknowledgement.

"It's time to leave here anyway; Banjica is next in line to be bombed or liberated, one of the two, and pity the poor prisoners if the bombs drop on them. Civilians are always the ones that pay the most in war."

Shayna releases a deep gasp in fear of the entire situation, "and my family?"

"Shayna, you must understand that all you can do is think positive and hope for the best. Thank God all your family is still alive."

Shayna smiles weakly, trying to give it her best hope, "and Albert?"

"Well, I must tell you; he's been sick a lot."

"Poor Albert, I love him too."

Wilhelm gazes with eyes fixed on Shayna.

"Did you forget that I'm married to him?"

"No, no I didn't forget, but someday, will we be married?"

Shayna buries her face into her son who still sits on her lap. "I don't know Wilhelm, but I must remember my vows to Albert. He has suffered so much in Banjica."

Officer Frolich looks away. "Alright Shayna, I must respect that because I respect you and we have a child together and two years have passed."

Shayna nods her head and changes the subject. "When are we leaving?"

"As soon as possible," Frolich is steadfast. "We can't fumble now."

CHAPTER FIFTY-ONE

ALBERT LIES ON his bed, unmoved and lackadaisical. Two Serbian guards enter and glare down at him. The first guard points his rifle at Albert's head. "Get up and go to work or you get a bullet."

Suddenly, war planes roar overhead swishing their hostile tails behind them like hawks homing in on their prey. The entire barracks shakes and shutters as their belligerent engines shatter any thought of further conversation. As their pupils dilate with panic, the two Serbian guards' faces fall cold and pale and their rifles wobble in their trembling hands. *How do you like it?* Albert snickers to himself in the deafening rumble.

As the war planes blast begins to fade and trail off, stillness drops. Albert unplugs his ears. Taken aback the guards remember where they are. Albert reaches up and pushes the rifle barrel away from his head. He turns over and sits up on the side of his bed as he thrusts himself to his feet, brushes the lint off of his clothes and stands at attention. He is ready for work blurting out his occasional humor at the expense of the Regimen. "Is that all I get at the end of a dead-end job, a bullet? Where's my gold watch?"

Shayna and Officer Frolich pack their bags for Landshut, Germany.

"Don't take too much luggage Shayna. We must travel light to make it look like we're coming back soon."

"Alright," Shayna fixes on him as fear seems to shoot through her body.

"Stay strong love, don't get weak. We must go through Austria and Germany both. You can't look frightened or the German patrols will know that something is wrong."

Shayna catches herself and tries to push it away, "Yes, yes, anything for little Thomas."

Albert and Murray stand alone and talk quietly among themselves in the main courtyard; a few of the remaining prisoners mill aimlessly around them. An uneasy anxiety fills the air and nerves are on edge as war planes have thundered numerous times overhead releasing their dark clouds of terror.

"So, is your health better now?" Murray tilts his head in Albert's direction.

"Yea, I guess for now."

"Watch what you eat and boil the water, that's very important in this diseased cesspool."

"Yes, I boil it." Albert repeats as he glances up toward the entrance.

As the gate opens a small covered military truck pulls out from the house behind the barracks and Officer Frolich drives it alone out onto the adjoining road. The gate guard closes the gate behind him. Albert and Murray both watch inquisitively as the truck drives away.

"What?" Albert's face starts to puff up red. "Now I know!"

Murray senses something challenging might be heading his way and he starts to prepare himself for the worst. "Know what Albert?"

"That's the bastard that got Shayna pregnant. The SS German Security Officer Frolich did it."

Murray jerks himself up to attention ready to control Albert if necessary. "Now Albert, just calm down, remember what we talked about and how you need to control your emotions?"

Albert guffaws. "I don't care anymore Murray."

"What?"

"You heard me; I don't really care anymore. I'm sick to death of all this insanity and bullshit, and all the murdering bastards and scum anyway."

Murray gapes at Albert in abject revelation.

Albert nods again and laughs out loud, "Really!"

Blinking his eyes in amazement, Murray stands back and assesses Albert as a new man.

"The Allied planes are coming soon! I hear them fly overhead all the time." Albert squints up to the sky in a reverie. "Finally, the planes will blow this hell hole into little pieces along with all the garbage and cockroaches that run it and think that they own the world and everyone in it."

CHAPTER FIFTY-TWO

OFFICER WILHELM FROLICH drives their small military truck through Austria. They continue plugging along heading toward Germany. Shayna and little Thomas ride shotgun with him. There is a sign posted along the road which reads: ENTERING GERMANY.

"So, this is Germany?" Shayna blinks uneasy.

"Yes, we are in the heart of it now." Officer Frolich can't help but smile, he is going home.

Shayna, Officer Frolich and Thomas sit and eat dinner at a private table toward the back of a small family restaurant in Germany. Shayna glances around her but doesn't say much or display any reactions. Thomas laughs and giggles, happy to be with his parents. Shayna and Officer Frolich take turns feeding him. They wipe his mouth as he slobbers and tries to blubber at the same time.

When they finish eating, the waitress presents the bill and collects the money from Officer Frolich. They gather up Thomas and climb back into their small truck ready to continue on their way toward the city of Landshut, Germany.

Shayna holds her son as he sleeps in her lap; she starts to doze off as well. Continuing on through Germany in the dark of early evening, Frolich carries on like a soldier driving the military truck without hesitation toward his goal of home.

"Let's find a place to sleep for the night Wilhelm. We need to clean up and take a shower. Thomas has food smeared all over his clothes, and he stinks."

"Fine, keep your eyes alert."

Out of nowhere a large German military truck follows them with flashing red lights. Shayna turns around to look, grabs Thomas and pulls him tight in fear. "What is it?"

"They want us to stop."

"What for?"

"I have no idea Shayna, but you must calm down or they'll think that something is wrong."

"Oh, no."

"Shayna, are you listening to me?"

Shayna glares at Frolich with her pupils dilated in wide-eyed excitement. She nods her head in affirmation.

"I want you to take a deep breath and think of little Thomas. Do you want anything to happen to our baby? They could take our child away from us and maybe even kill him."

"No, of course not," Shayna snaps at him viciously.

"Please!" Wilhelm speaks in a hushed tone avoiding any direct eye contact with Shayna.

"Okay, okay," Shayna takes a deep breath and holds it while closing her eyes and doing her best to drive away the fear.

"My dad always said that life is merely a hope for less pain and a wish for tranquility."

"I'll make that wish." Shayna tries to smile.

Officer Frolich pulls his truck over to the side of the road. The large German military truck pulls up behind him with its headlights glaring into their truck. Frolich looks over at Shayna unruffled. "Are you okay?"

Shayna bobs her head yes, and kisses Thomas who is still asleep on her lap. Wilhelm puts on his German military hat and his Swastika arm band. Two large German soldiers get out of the truck and walk towards them. The soldiers are dressed appropriately in military uniforms with accompanying swastika arm bands. Officer Frolich rolls down his window. The soldier on Wilhelm's side approaches his window while the other soldier stands guard several feet away, surveying the situation. They speak in German.

"Gutenabend, soldat "(Good evening soldier). The first German soldier greets Officer Frolich.

"S.S. Offizer Wilhelm Frolich hier herr, vom Banjica-Lager in Jugoslawien" (SS Officer Wilhelm Frolich here sir, from the Banjica Camp in Yugoslavia).

The first soldier signals acceptance to Officer Frolich, and then bends down looking past Frolich into the truck at Shayna and little Thomas. Shayna smiles at him. He nods back in return.

"Kann ich aus dem Lastwagen herauskommen?" (Can I get out of the truck?) Officer Frolich asks respectfully.

The first soldier bends his head in affirmation and steps back out of the way. Officer Frolich climbs out of his truck. All three Germans walk away from Frolich's truck and talk privately in German. They speak quietly with each other and confirm Officer Frolich.

Ten minutes later Wilhelm moves back into his truck. The German soldiers continue to stand behind his tuck. Shayna glances at Frolich who briefly smiles at her giving her a secret hand signal that everything is alright. Shayna swallows hard and heaves out a long-held sigh of relief.

"Relax love," Frolich requests of her. "Someone painted 'NAZI ASSHOLE' in white letters on the back of our truck."

Shayna drops back into her seat and releases her strangling grip on Thomas who she would have gladly given her life to keep from the German soldiers if need be.

"Just sit tight while the nice German soldiers scrap it off."

"But, when did that happen?"

"Some war resisters probably did it while we were in the restaurant eating dinner."

"In Germany?" Shayna reels in astonishment.

"Yes, I'm afraid so." Officer Frolich lightly concurs with a sigh of his own release as the truck rattles and rolls and the antiwar graffiti is scrapped into oblivion.

After the incident with the German soldiers, Frolich is immediately on the road again. He appears spent and weary. "Shayna, we need to pull over and get some sleep and like you said, take a shower."

"Fine, but is everything alright now, you don't look so well?"

Officer Frolich rambles and pulls the truck over to the side of the road while the engine runs. He leaves on the warning lights to avoid being hit. Thomas lies asleep.

Frolich drops his head onto the steering wheel. "What is it Wilhelm?"

Frolich abruptly and unexpectedly folds his hands over his face in an act of proxy weeping. "That is exactly what I am, a Nazi Asshole!"

Shayna is aghast. "What? Why would you say that?"

"Because I'm a hypocrite, I hate the Nazi ideology, and always, always, I have to salute Heil Hitler... Sieg Heil just like a stupid, ignorant asshole."

Shayna scrunches up her mouth as if searching for just the right answer.

"Every day I have to look at that bloated Commandant. Yes sir, No sir, I'm an idiot." Shayna bites her lip giving up on words and knowing what is finally coming out is the truth. "Friedrich reminds me of a big, ugly tape worm sucking out people's blood, I hate him!" Shayna gapes at Wilhelm, stunned.

"And that low-life scum Vujkovic, he's just a parasitic wasp that lays its eggs in caterpillars, buries them paralyzed and then sucks out their hapless lives leaving them a shell to dry up and die."

Shayna falls back horrified with Frolich's enraged outbursts.

"And Hitler, if that moron only knew how much educated Germans hate his guts, he never even finished high school; he's a drop out, a quitter. He's losing the war because he's too dim witted to listen to his generals, and all the disenfranchised fools and losers that think he's God, follow blindly along behind him doing his dastardly deeds because they think that he will make them rich."

Shayna gives up now and lets Wilhelm continue with his rant, hoping that it will end soon. Little Thomas starts to stir and smack his lips for food.

"Rich Germans don't need the Jews money because they have their own," Frolich rages on. Thomas starts to babble picking up on his dad's irritations and disappointments.

"Blast Hitler! Germany's blown to hell again with a psycho behind the wheel! World War I wasn't bad enough, now we let a raving lunatic do it again." Frolich fumes, red faced like a furnace finally blasting it all out.

Thomas starts to cry and then wail, just like his dad.

Albert lies in bed in his barracks. Two Serbian State guards enter. Before they can speak in their signature droll delivery, Albert shouts out at them. "I got the craps, go away."

The first guard orders Albert, "You must come to work now!"

"Okay, just a minute then," Albert dumps himself out of his bunk. "Gotta take a crap first, okay? Then you both can carry me to the bank barracks, but I don't think that there's any toilet paper left. You can still carry me, wiped off or not, okay?"

Both Serbian guards glare in disbelief at Albert as he crawls across the floor on hands and knees, too weak and dehydrated to stand. Screams of pain and release come from the toilet area. The guards leave.

The small house is partially covered with trees and shrubs as it hides itself in the Yugoslavian mountains making it a perfect hideout and shelter for partisans or wanted Rebel Generals.

Partisan Commander Josip Broz Tito and General Moshe Piade, both with monetary rewards on their heads, sit at a handmade wooden table and eat dinner followed by a few drinks, and then a good night's sleep before the shooting and bombs start again.

"The Belgrade Offensive is beginning soon, and we will lose many good men to it." Commander Tito speaks with the sorrow of war.

"Yes Tito, but it's time for the Germans to leave Belgrade and get out of the Balkans altogether." Major General Piade of the Yugoslav People's Army holds strong.

Commander Tito stares at General Piade for a moment in a hard acceptance. "We've spent our lives fighting the oppressors, in and out of jail for years as political prisoners."

General Piade bangs his open hand on the wooden table. "What kind of life is that?"

"But I know no life other than the military; I will die in the military." Commander Tito knows who he is.

"Death for freedom doesn't scare me anymore Tito." General Piade looks to the windows and the diligent rays of late evening light still beaming their way in, free as the air.

CHAPTER FIFTY-THREE

SHAYNA AND WILHELM pull into the driveway of an upper middle-class home in Landshut, Germany. Shayna is silent and fretful as Wilhelm parks the truck.

"Relax love, you and our little guy will live here," Wilhelm motions finally smiling.

"Oh, but I... I"

Wilhelm interrupts her bumbling. "My mother will help you with her only grandchild. I never told you Shayna, but I'm an only child."

"Wonderful." Shayna replies deciding not to speak further.

Thomas tight in Shayna's arms, she climbs out of the truck and walks up to the door of the house with Wilhelm. His mother, Mrs. Forlich, opens the screen door appearing to have seen the truck pull up. She is in her mid-sixties and wears a plain house dress seeming to be a woman of no nonsense or airs. "Oh Wilhelm," Mrs. Frolich smiles and hugs her son. "It's so wonderful to see you. I've missed you so much."

"Mother, this is Shayna and this little boy is our child." Wilhelm takes Thomas out of Shayna's arms and holds him in his as he introduces Thomas to his Grandmother Frolich.

Astonished, Mrs. Frolich stands with her eyes wide-open and her arms dangling at her side like an immobile puppet. "What? What Wilhelm, we have a grandchild? Oh, I never thought it would happen so soon. Your father will be so happy." Mrs. Frolich touches little Thomas and almost tears with joy. She then turns to mama Shayna and extends her hand.

"Very nice to meet you Mrs. Frolich," Shayna says and returns the handshake. Mrs. Frolich smiles at her good manners.

Without containing himself, Wilhelm interrupts any further talk.

"How is Dad anyway?"

Mrs. Frolich's happiness is short lived as she withdraws a bit. "Not so good Wilhelm."

"Mother, I'm so sorry."

"The doctors say that your father is dying because he's bedridden with heart problems."

"That's not a medical diagnosis." Wilhelm lets out a guffaw of confusion.

"Such a wonderful kind man and he has to go before his time because of this dreadful war."

Wilhelm takes his mother's hand. "We'll just see about all this diagnosis nonsense."

Mrs. Frolich smiles encouragingly at Wilhelm with a newfound strength. "But just maybe, this good news of a grandchild might bring your dad's health and happiness back again, with a renewed reason for living."

Prime Minister, Sir Winston Churchill appears in public in London. "We will never, ever surrender to Hitler." A bellow of applause blasts out from every British civilian left standing.

Somewhere hidden in the Yugoslavian mountains lays the Balkan Air Force Base. The landing strip is surrounded by trees and brush making it a secrecy that the Germans haven't discovered yet. Allied planes come and go dropping off food supplies and war munitions for the partisans and picking up the wounded rebels for medical treatment.

Partisan Commander Joseph Broz Tito and General Moshe Piade stand in front of a British military plane. Both men enter the plane and the doors close behind them clinching a final acceptance of the partisans by British military forces. The British will now stand behind the partisans, giving them planes, tanks and scores of various munitions as well as medical help in an agreeable partnership. This will determine the final outcome of the war against Germany in the Balkans.

The British military plane takes off, blasting air as it roars like a lion carrying the united hope and survival of an entire generation of suppressed people as it disappears into the blue sky.

Albert lies in his bed, his legs raised toward his chest in a semi-fetal position. There's no future here in this demoralizing institution, they've reduced me into an animated robot, I can't help anyone anymore and there's no escaping this hell hole, he mulls over in his mind.

Two Serbian guards enter Albert's cell.

Albert looks up. "I don't feel so well, got the craps again from your contaminated water." Albert reasons, *My body can't fight this putrefied water because I'm so down in the dumps.*

"You will come to work!" The first guard gives the order pointing his rifle at Albert. There is an awkward silence as if the guards aren't actually sure of their power.

"Work? What for?" Albert quizzes picking up on their indecisiveness and ignoring the rifle barrel, not in an act of submission but in an act of total apathy. "I just sit there all day anyway and do nothing. There's no more money or goods for me to transfer. All the Jews are dead because you criminals stole their money and then killed them!"

"Except for you!" The second guard raises his rifle also at Albert making the threat as clear as a schoolboy can understand. Both guards look at each other and laugh.

Albert is tired and drained as he can only stare up in helplessness at their cruel amusements and mortal threats. "Just go ahead and shoot me," Albert releases in his despair.

The two guards glare down at Albert, enjoying his misery momentarily from above like vampires feeding on it in a sick vicarious game of dominance and submission.

"Do you think I'm kidding? Go ahead and shoot me! Go ahead!" Albert inevitably loses his ability to feel fear. His mind seems to switch it off with hopelessness as he drains to himself. *My life means nothing now, so I can say whatever I want.*

The guards stagger deathly quiet giving up their false supremacy, hesitating at their new challenge. They stand dazed and not quite sure of the scope of their orders, or if Administrator Vujkovic or the Commandant would approve of them murdering Albert the Banker or not. They clown around with each other in uncertainty, take a few steps backward and then gradually lower their rifles as though giving up the argument in order to save their own hides.

"I'm not the banker any longer, retired or dead. I just don't care anymore, about anything." Albert lets out his truth like a leaky water faucet. *My life or death will not change anything,* he believes, *and I know now that shock is a survival technique brewed up by a person's own mind to keep them from themselves.*

The two guards abandon their macho at their own discretion as if it was just another hat to toss and laugh again in enjoyment at Albert's heartache and isolation. They turn around and then leave, snickering and joking as they go.

CHAPTER FIFTY-FOUR

THE DAY IS September 14, 1944, the first day of the Belgrade Strategic Offensive. The Allied forces of the Soviet Red Army, Tito's Rebel Partisans and the Bulgarian People's Army prepare to attack the city of Belgrade to drive out the occupied Germans and Serbian forces. They have been warned and given the surrender option but refuse to relinquish the city.

Military tanks enter Belgrade as Allied planes drop bombs on occupied Germans and mostly the Serbian military. Gunshots ring out as grenades explode killing not only Axis forces, unfortunately inhabiting innocent civilians and injuring Allied soldiers as well. This well laid out invasion and mortal fighting continues until October 20th of the same year.

Bella, Walter and Mimi stand outside and watch the clouds of dark smoke drift by everyday coming from the city of Belgrade. The Allied planes continue to fly over Banjica creating a constant and dangerous war zone. Axis desertion is now common in Banjica as the impending doom of Allied attack looms each day, blasting and smoldering overhead.

Bella, Walter and Mimi quickly disappear into their bungalows behind the locked gate.

As the Belgrade Strategic Offensive winds down toward Allied victory, the Banjica camp is liberated during the first week of October by Tito's Rebel Partisans. One hundred Yugoslav partisans swarm the mostly abandoned camp and liberate those who remain, shooting the remaining livid German and Serbian guards who know that their power will be worthless if the war ends. They will have to face unemployment and personal devastation again because most are uneducated, unskilled or just plain lazy.

The remaining hundred Jewish, mixed Slavic and Serbian civilian prisoners' revolt and join in the fight. They fight against the remaining egotistically deranged guards who refuse to accept the final impending realization that Hitler is losing the war.

Murray is with Albert who is amazingly still alive, but not yet recuperated from his depression and chronic diarrhea and looks generally wasted in the morning light of his bunk. An oppressive shadow drains his life away filling the cell block with the heaviness of stale humid air. Albert ponders to himself; *I once was certain that I could escape this pit, but that self-concocted lie has abandoned me just like my inner lawyer.*

"I'm going out to the battle." Murray picks up his rifle.

"What's going on out there Murray?" Albert stares with an absent look on his face.

"The partisan rebels have stormed the camp. I'm going out to fight for our freedom."

Murray scrutinizes as Albert immediately relinquishes his vacancy and strains to lift himself up from his bed the best he can. He holds his stomach leaning over. "Give me a rifle too."

Murray shakes his head no. "You're too weak to fight!"

"Damn it, give me a rifle, I gotta go kill those murdering guards, and find the Commandant. I'm gonna shoot that bastard too."

"I will not! Your half dead right now, you don't have any military training and you'll just get yourself killed!"

With the rush of an adrenaline burst, Albert flies at Murray kicking and scratching and attempts to seize his rifle. After a short, futile struggle Albert gathers himself to do battle without a rifle. "They murdered my family. My entire family is dead because of them. I will shoot them!" Albert shrieks like he's back from the grave.

Murray grabs Albert and attempts to lead him back to his bed without another struggle. "Let me go out! Let me go fight!" Albert thrashes and shoves to get past Murray, but Murray forcefully holds him back. Albert then slumps to the floor worn out with heavy, labored breathing.

Murray makes sure that Albert has passed out in his bed and then picks up his rifle and goes out into the main courtyard to fight.

He finds the struggle is over and the silent camp is littered with dead and wounded men. All the German and Serbian guards lie dead with multiple bullet wounds. Yugoslav partisans carry wounded men away on stretchers and put them into an open military truck.

Albert suddenly appears in the courtyard. Murray rushes to him and leads him toward a military truck which displays the sign: RED CROSS. " I'll go with you for medical attention Albert. It's set up near the synagogue on the outskirts of Belgrade."

"Thank you, Murray, for everything."

"We'll leave soon. Can you make it to the Red Cross truck on your own?"

Albert forces a balance somewhere between hope and horror, "no problem."

"I'll be back in a few minutes. Don't let them leave without me, okay Albert?"

Albert nonverbally motions in acknowledgment. Murray then leaves to check up on his wife and son in the back house.

As Albert limps toward the truck, he passes two dead German guards face up on the ground. They still hold their rifles clutched in their fists ultimately waiting for action even in death. A stunned stillness takes over Albert as though he is preparing for the charge of battle and a vein of violent emotions carries him further. A low guttural shriek accompanied by a malicious grimace takes over his face and he sneers like Jingo. Quivering with rage and a soul retching fury, Albert screeches with the ultimate animosity and vengeance of a wrongly punished man. Albert the deranged lunatic waves his boney arms in the air. "You scum! You garbage! You started all this... Death to the Fuhrer! Death to the Fuhrer!"

Totally out of reason and control, Albert falls to the ground and wrestles the rifle away from one of the dead German guard's hand, jumps up in a death threat, and shoots both of the dead German guards again and again until one muscle bound Partisan comes to comfort him. The Partisan is eventually forced to slap Albert in the face for safety reasons as he tries to grapple the rifle away from him. "No! No!" Albert screams still clinging to the rifle. "They killed my entire family!"

Albert's face is frozen in a madman's twist as the rifle is finally jerked away from him.

CHAPTER FIFTY-FIVE

MURRAY WALKS TOWARD the house behind the barracks. Bella, Walter and Mimi watch as Murray approaches the chain-link fence. Mimi opens the lock on the gate and Murray comes through it as Walter runs up and hugs him, "Dad, Dad!" Murray checks Walter over, "Boy oh boy, you have grown! Look how tall you are now!"

Murray then turns and goes to Bella and they hug. Both have tears in their eyes. "I don't know how we made it through this nightmare Murray. God help those who had it worse off than we did. God bless those who were tortured and killed."

Murray blinks his eyes and nods in total agreement in a moment of respect for the dead, then relinquishing. "I must go with the wounded now before the truck leaves."

Bella releases him. "Fine, please go help them."

"Albert's dehydrated and out of his mind. He needs treatment desperately."

"Just go Murray. We'll be here when you get back." Bella smiles satisfied.

Mimi grins and wipes the tears of joy from her eyes. "We'll all be here waiting for you." Murray nods politely to Mimi and shakes her hand. "Thank you for taking care of my family and God bless you too!"

Mimi smiles and blushes a bit in her old lady polite dignity. "Thank you, Mr. Weinberg." Bella goes over and hugs Mimi. "Yes, God bless you Mimi." Mimi is beyond joyous.

Murray then turns and hurries back toward the gate. "Be sure to lock this because there will be dangerous people out and about tonight." Murray waves goodbye to Walter, and he waves back in return, but then Murray abruptly halts remembering something important. "Just one more thing ladies. There is a loaded gun in the kitchen drawer of the main house if you need it and please don't hesitate to use it if totally necessary." Both women gawk at each other as if they've never touched a gun in their life. "Remember, just in case of extreme danger, okay?" Murray is adamant.

Mimi holds up the key and shakes it in acknowledgement. "We certainly will lock that gate and shoot the criminals if necessary, too."

Murray sits in the back of the Red Cross truck trying to comfort all the wounded men with their injuries and pleas for help. Albert is passed out with his mouth hanging open as he mumbles to himself in his deep and disturbing sleep.

CHAPTER FIFTY-SIX

OFFICER WILHELM FROLICH opens his father's bedroom door and walks in. Mr. Frolich is bedridden but looks up and smiles with the fresh air and sunshine coming through an open window. Mr. Frolich stretches out his boney arm and hand to his son, "Wilhelm, Wilhelm."

Wilhelm walks over and sits in the chair next to his father's bed. He reaches out taking his father's hand and returns the smile in encouragement.

"Hi dad, you have a grandchild now, his name is Thomas."

Shayna, Wilhelm, Mrs. Frolich and Thomas sit in the dining room and eat lunch.

"I heard on the radio that the Banjica Camp has been liberated and all the inmates are free." Wilhelm nonchalantly mentions.

Shayna is startled and then he regrets his ill timing. "What?" Shayna looks up at him pushing back the tears.

Mrs. Frolich stares at Shayna with questions in her eyes.

"Mother, Shayna had neighbors who were taken to the Banjica Camp."

"Oh, how terrible, I'm so sorry Shayna." Mrs. Frolich gives Shayna a look of support.

Shayna and Wilhelm sit on the sofa alone. Thomas plays with toys near them. "You saved my family's lives Wilhelm."

"No Shayna, you saved your family, not me, and now they will save themselves."

"If Banjica is liberated, where will you report for duty?"

"Probably to that horrible Jasenovac Concentration Camp in Croatia. It's open for business as usual and I hear that there are some really deranged, savage guards there."

"Don't they ever stop?"

Wilhelm bends his head toward her and shakes it in the negative. "You must not tell anyone, not even my mother that you are not German. "

Shayna stares at him in question.

"If the German Army finds out our secret, they will come here and kill everyone, including our little boy Thomas."

Shayna's face falls with complete dread. "Can't you just stay here with us?"

"That would make me a deserter and they would come looking for me."

Shayna holds with her alarm and dread.

"If I don't come back, you can live here with my mother until the war is over."

"What Wilhelm? Why wouldn't you come back?"

Shayna, Mrs. Frolich and toddler Thomas stand out front as Wilhelm backs his covered military truck out of the driveway. He waves goodbye to them and they wave back in apprehension as he drives off, back into the war zone.

CHAPTER FIFTY-SEVEN

MURRAY, BELLA, MIMI and about twenty other Jews, ethnic Slavs and civilian Serbs gather near the entrance of Banjica. Murray speaks out to the group. "I know that Banjica is closed, but my wife and I are going to stay near the camp until the war officially ends because, well, we might not even have a house left."

The small crowd talks among themselves.

"Whatever you do or wherever you go, I urge you to be very careful because there are those out there who would deliberately hurt you. The Jasenovac Concentration Camp is still open and active."

A loud gasp of horror rings out in unison.

"Jasenovac is controlled by even worse guards than we had here in Banjica, so please take care and don't trust anyone that you don't know."

"But winter is coming." A man yells from the crowd.

"Yes, I know, so you must plan carefully and use all resources available. The Red Cross and other agencies will be available to help you with shelter and food until spring."

A military truck pulls up. Albert gets out of it with a water bottle clutched in his hand. Murray waves to him and Albert approaches the small crowd.

Bella flashes a smile of warm welcome. "Albert, you're well, thank God!"

Albert smiles back at her. "Yes, I am, and thank you for noticing."

Albert hugs Bella and shakes Murray and Walter's hands, then drops Walter's hand and gives him a big hug while picking him up off the ground. "Put me down, put me down." Everyone laughs and

Albert lowers Walter to the ground again. "I'm not a little kid anymore," Walter demands swishing his body in a macho posture.

Albert laughs, as something in the near distance catches his eye and he energetically focuses on it in absolute amazement. A bright yellow dandelion grows in a cement crack outside of the main courtyard. It blows and swings happily in the warm fall breeze all-encompassing in nature's pure power, proud and majestic and happy to be alive.

Albert sways his body. *I'm feeling lightheaded like I might faint or something,* Albert swirls to himself. Suddenly he is aware of a bright white light encircling the yellow flower. The bright light instantly moves into Albert's head and his body is flushing and vibrantly surrounded by this same intense white light. Still standing, Albert lets his head fall back and closes his eyes. He is stunned momentarily with the healing power and forces of the pure white light.

Albert lets out an electrically charged breath and finally opens his eyes. The bright light slowly fades away as Albert smiles with joy, happiness, and a renewed energy he hasn't felt for several years. *Oh my God, what just happened to me?* Albert stands tall and examines himself. *Do I still have arms and legs?*

"Albert, Albert," Bella motions to him anxiously, "Are you alright?"

Albert smiles with a new uplifting radiance and vision. Bella rushes over to Albert to help him in any way possible.

"Bella, I'm okay, thank you so much for all your help."

"Well, okay, you're very welcome Albert."

"I don't really know what just happened to me, but I felt like I was in the eye of the storm and now I can see clearly again. It's like a miracle just happened to me, like the war is finally over." Albert can't quit smiling. His face is calm, and his demons seem exorcised as he holds the tranquility of one who maybe feels at ease in his own skin again. *It's like I just experienced a direct link with the divine and immediately became one with it,* Albert remembers. *I felt a surge of life as though I were given a great gift of the power of pure love pumping through me.*

"You left us for a while there, I thought you were going to faint." Bella is a mother and responds appropriately so.

"Bella, I just found my inner wolf of peace and tranquility. I felt my boundaries and judgments disappear like I was suspended in happiness and pleasantly released from the physical world."

Bella puts her hand up to her mouth as if *tell me no lie,* amazing. Murray is speechless. Albert walks over and pours water out of his bottle onto the yellow dandelion. "With all the horrible things going on in Banjica, this flower is still alive."

"That's just a weed!" Walter yells all knowingly. "Pull it up! It doesn't deserve to live!" Bella and Murray gape at Walter in total and utter astonishment.

Albert gives a fixed stare of newfound distress at Walter, but then releases a deep breath and calms down knowing that Walter is still just a kid. It doesn't matter how much he pretends to be a well-adjusted adult.

"Walter, that's what the Germans said about us, that we didn't deserve to live. No one should play God." Albert waits for Walter's reaction in anticipation and education.

Walter eyes both of his parents expecting their approval of his remark, but they glare back at him in the bewilderment of disapproval and a looming lecture. Walter glances over at Albert again as Albert rattles his head in a dissatisfied no. Walter then flicks his eyes away, looking down at the ground absolutely ashamed of himself.

CHAPTER FIFTY-EIGHT

IT IS APRIL of 1945 and Jasenovac Concentration Camp is liberated by Tito's Partisans. Italy's Dictator Benito Mussolini, who supports Jasenovac, is also executed by Italian partisans in the same month of April. Hitler commits suicide soon after knowing that he has lost the war and that he will be disgraced and humiliated with a similar public execution. Unfortunately, his dog Blondie goes down with him at his own hands as if the shepherd's own innate innocence is somehow joined in with his master's evil karma.

Albert and the Weinberg family have somehow made it through the winter with the help of social services. With Germany's official surrender only days away, they make their way back toward their former houses. Hitching rides and carrying minimal baggage, a small military truck pulls up, stops, and they all jump on, riding it until they reach their final destination.

Bella, Murray, Walter and Albert stand in front of the Weinberg house and look up. On the outside the German troops have run it into the ground; the porch and yard are in total ruins. "Let's go inside and see the damages." Bella laments in casual acceptance as she walks up to the front door, opens it without any problem and goes inside as the others follow uneasily behind her as if an enemy soldier might suddenly be waiting with a rifle.

The interior is totally in shambles as well and what's left of her antique furniture is crushed and vandalized. Empty beer bottles lay everywhere with used food wrappers and rotting chicken bones. Maggots crawl on and around the bones smelling up the thick, musty mold filled air. Several windows are broken out and holes are punched in the walls from angry fists flying through with the indignation of a lost war.

"Is this where we live now?" Walter turns up his nose as if he's too good to walk through. Bella looks at Walter with a pitiful scowl seemingly wondering if he really is her son. She reflects if he has learned anything the entire time in Banjica. "Yes Walter," Bella holds it back for now. "We will start all over again."

Albert and Murray sit down on some wooden boxes left by the German soldiers. More than a touch of gloom falls on the household as they glance about at the devastation. The house's ethereal pulsations and vibrations of ruthlessness and acts of violence still cling to it as if a ghost of indiscretions past could appear at any moment. Bella finally stands up and begins to clean up the chicken bones first. "Blessings to our home and out with all the depression and evil spirits. We're all still alive and thank you God for that." Everyone joins in with a 'hurrah'.

"More than I can say for that chicken. Now I can identify with its death," Albert lets loose.

A moment of silence ensues with mention of the word *death*.

"So, where's Shayna now?" Albert throws in offhandedly as if trying to disguise his pain.

Bella winces, "Oh Albert, I'm so very sorry but, she lives in Landshut, Germany with her young son."

Albert immediately looks away.

"Albert, you must accept the unfortunate circumstances that if Walter and I had stayed in the woman's barracks, we would have died from starvation and typhoid too," Bella admits it.

Albert gapes in fixation at Bella trying to accept her words as they fly around and attempt to sink in.

Silence.

Albert finally speaks, "I'm going by my family's house to see if it's still there."

"Good!" Murray jumps in, "I'll go with you."

"But first I'm going to look for my dad and brother, they may still be alive."

"We'll go into Belgrade. A survivor's bureau has been set up there." Murray adds giving Albert hope and support.

"I'll go too," Bella agrees. "I hear there's a care center there and it's passing out food, sanitary supplies and used clothing."

Everyone smiles.

Silence again.

"How do you justify evil men like Jingo?" Albert searches for an answer.

"Albert," Murray attempts to placate him. "People die because war isn't an everyday happening and it always has its price."

Albert hangs on to his stillness.

"There is no standardized test to learn how to murder. Murders are mostly committed by laypersons, or hunters who just love to kill, that is unless you're a Nazi soldier and then you can get in a lot of justice free target practice."

"So, then I guess evil will always be with us?"

"Yes, but the egos of the world eventually run out of hot air and, unfortunately, someone near them just steps up to take their place."

"So then, regardless, I'm still master of my own fate, is that what you're trying to say?"

"Right Albert, but tell us again about what happened to you, like you said, in the white light of the flower?"

"To put it simply folks, I just found the miraculous in the mundane or the sublime in the ordinary and it was up to me to interpret it correctly. It didn't make me God, just an instrument thereof."

"What? I don't get it." Walter mumbles, assuming that it makes no sense.

Albert laughs with Walter. "Well Walter, neither do I, but whatever you wish to call me, madman or prophet, it makes no difference because we are one and the same. My madness was a wall between me and the evil world and just as music dissolves into time, I dissolve into the conflicted everyman." And with that, Albert walks out the door.

"Huh?" Walter scrunches up his face.

They all watch him go in bewilderment and sorrow not knowing exactly what they should say to Albert about what happened to his family or how they should feel about Bella's survival and Albert's sisters and their children dying in the same women's barracks that Bella and Walter escaped from with Shayna's help. "We'll give it to God to sort out," Bella sadly states.

"There is no other way, God bless the dead and may they rest in peace." Murray agrees almost with a sacrament and falls into a respectful moment of reverence.

Reflection penetrates the mood.

"Poor guy," Bella sympathizes but holds her dignity. "He's been through so, so much."

"He's changed." Murray grins with some satisfaction. "He isn't so obsessed with our Shayna anymore. The war forced him to grow up, and fast."

"Murray, we can't think about the war and all the horrible things that happened at Banjica or we will lose our minds."

"Yes Bella, you're right, let's be positive."

A shifting calm now fills the room as Murray fidgets appearing to sense something new is brewing.

"Murray, we have a grandchild. You're a grandpa now."

Murray gathers up a blank expression for Bella as if locked in solitude of things past and not so happily ever after remembered.

CHAPTER FIFTY-NINE

ON MAY 7, 1945 the German Wehrmacht (Nazi War Machine) unconditionally surrenders. The following day, May 8, 1945 is V-E Day and Germany signs in Berlin, officially surrendering.

Albert and the Weinbergs hitch a ride to the Belgrade Jewish Synagogue the next day. A sign out front reads: Jewish Agency for Palestine. They all walk toward the door cautiously with awe and disbelief that they might actually be dreaming and are still at Banjica.

Once through the door the trepidation dispenses and fortuity smiles on them in the shape of a large sign in front of them which reads: Survivor's Registration – World Jewish Congress. Several people weep and hug each other. Albert watches them in exhilaration yet filled with a dread that he will never see his dad and brother again. *That is just what Hitler wanted when he said that no one will ever remember the Holocaust or what happened there or much less care and I have to fight this ignorance and hatred, so I will go forward.* Albert projects not letting doubt, intimidation or apathy take him as he stands at attention for a moment gathering up his stamina and pushing back his sorrow. He then walks forward to register.

Across from the Survivor's Registration is another large sign which reads: United Nations Relief Administration – food, clothes & supplies. Bella, Murray and Walter stand in line as refugee war survivors and wait their turn.

CHAPTER SIXTY

THERE IS A loud knock on the front door of the Frolich house in Landshut, Germany. Mrs. Frolich walks from the kitchen and through the living room to answer it. Shayna and Thomas sit in the living room. Shayna reads a book and Thomas plays with a toy truck.

Wilhelm walks into the living room. He is dressed in dirty street rags and is barely recognizable with smudges of dried mud caked on his face, overgrown beard and brushy mustache. He limps on his left foot and his right arm is in a tattered sling. Shayna glares at him in shock. Thomas runs and hides behind the sofa as if the monster in his favorite kiddy book has just walked in.

Mrs. Frolich tears, "Wilhelm, we were all so worried about you. It's been eight months since we've heard from you." Mrs. Frolich and Wilhelm hug each other.

"I know mother, I stink, and I've been beaten up, but I'm still alive."

"You're going to the hospital immediately. I'm going to get the car out of the garage now!"

"I want to take a shower first mother, please, just look at me, and the horrible smell?"

"Okay my darling son, I will get you some fruit juice to pep you up first."

Wilhelm emerges from his bedroom showered and in clean clothes, but he is still dehydrated and weak. "I need to rest mother, please let me."

"No, you can rest at the hospital. I won't have you dying on me here at home." Wilhelm relents in agreement meaning that he can attempt to do no more. "I'll get the car out of the garage now! Meet me out front!" Wilhelm almost faints onto the floor and Mrs. Frolich gives him a hand. "You go out front with Shayna, she will help you to stand up and I will tell your dad that we're leaving and then I'll lock the door!"

"Okay mother, dad's still with us?"

"Yes, he sees Thomas every day and he's much better with a grandchild around." Mrs. Frolich is curt and brisk as she walks toward her husband's bedroom.

Shayna stands up from the sofa and goes to Wilhelm and they hug unsure of their feelings toward each other after so much separation and tragedy.

"We thought that you were captured by the partisans, Wilhelm."

Wilhelm regards Shayna for an apprehensive moment as if choking up some intense emotions and then frowns down at the floor in a distant haze. He bites his bottom lip seeming to be holding some heartbreak back that he really doesn't want to remember. "I was a prisoner-of-war for a while when the partisans liberated Jasenovac."

"What happened to you?" Shayna asks what she shouldn't at an ill-gotten time.

Wilhelm looks away and trembles in sorrow and then in terror as if the rifles are going off in his head again and the invisible walls of the past close in on him. Wilhelm is in the Jasenovac Concentration Camp before the arrival of the partisans and a civilian has tipped off the Croatian guards that the partisans are near and will soon be upon them.

"No!" SS Officer Wilhelm Frolich orders the first Croatian guard. "Don't burn down the camp!" The guard pushes Officer Frolich aside, gathers up the other guards and begins to torch all the buildings in Jasenovac. "Stop this arson! Stop! That is an order!" Officer Frolich shouts at them. The Croatian guards gang up on Frolich and beat him unconscious to the ground. When Frolich wakes up, smoke engulfs him and flames bellow in approach. In a fit of coughing and crawling on his hands and knees, he drags himself out of the camp.

Once outside, Officer Frolich finds himself prey yet again. "Get your hands off of me!" Frolich screeches, but the partisan rebels now have him and pull him up to his feet giving over to several other rebels who lead him away at gunpoint. Still wearing his German SS uniform, Officer Frolich is easy quarry and falls to the ground yet again exhausted and bleeding, but the partisans beat and kick him as loud rifle fires and bombs deafen his ears.

The next day Officer Wilhelm Frolich wakes up on a pile of dirt and dusty ground. *What's happening to me?* He recalls now as he rubs the clouds out of his swollen eyes with the back of his filthy blood-stained hands and looks through the barbwire fence of a prisoner-of-war camp. All around him are hundreds of other men just like him. Some are in German military uniforms and others of Serbian descent lay on the ground but dressed in their own special guard uniforms giving them away as the enemy. Frolich thrusts his red stained and burned clothes aside, stands up in a ragged white undershirt and as his hands grab the chain-link fence, he pushes his broken face into it. Frolich lets the words rush out. "I want out of here, now!" He urgently rattles the heavy fence.

The other prisoners just stare at him with their own brand of madness. Thoughts of when Albert was at his gate banging his head, seep back through his memories, but he shoves them out and continues with the fence banging. "Let me out, let me out!" Wilhelm's shrieks are audible now and Shayna steps back in fright seriously regretting what she has asked him.

"I am so sorry, so sorry. I won't ask anything more about the war." Shayna trembles in alarm as she holds Wilhelm up.

A car honks from the driveway and lingers somewhere in Wilhelm's head. *Where am I?* He shudders, looking around for the fence.

"Thomas and I will go to the hospital with you Wilhelm, okay?"

"What?" Wilhelm nods his head affirmatively seeming to finally realize that he is at his parent's house.

"I'm so sorry Wilhelm, but I must know now about my family. Did you see my family?"

"Shayna?"

"Yes, it's me Shayna."

"Well... so I hear from ex-prisoners, they're all still alive," Wilhelm moans in pain. Without another word, Shayna gasps and holds her hands over her mouth in happiness. "I hear they're all back in your house in Yugoslavia... refugees now."

"And, what about Albert?"

"Albert... guess he's still kicking too, so I hear."

Shayna and Wilhelm's eyes meet in deep question and worry as they gaze intently at each other unsure of where their lives will go now that the war is over.

The horn honks again outside.

CHAPTER SIXTY-ONE

BELLA HAS DONE wonders with her ramshackle house and it stands halfway decent again.

A letter is delivered into their new mailbox. Albert stands and watches through a window as the carrier's mailbag disappears and then he goes out to get the mail. He pulls out a letter addressed to him, opens it, and reads slowly. Awe drops down his face as he ambles back into the Weinberg home.

Bella meets Albert coming back in and he hands her the letter. Bella reads it as her mouth tightens first in conjecture, then in astonishment and finally in question. "It's from Shayna?"

"Yea, she's coming for a visit and bringing her son Thomas." Albert holds back.

"I can hardly believe it." Delight and joy now push out any doubt in Bella's expression.

Albert appears very pleased but remains on his guard. "She promised me that she would see me again after the war was over, and it looks like she's keeping her word."

"Oh," Bella scrunches up her smile, "just her son, right?"

"Yes, she's bringing just her son." Albert laughs at the thought of Officer Frolich trailing along behind her like a puppy dog. He smiles again and goes into his bedroom, shutting the door behind him.

There is a loud knock on the Weinberg's front door. Bella opens the door, gawking at Shayna standing there holding her four-year-old son, Thomas, by the hand.

"Shayna, Shayna," Bella grabs her long-lost daughter and hugs her endlessly. Shayna and Thomas come into the living room and Murray appears in high spirits.

"Hi dad," Shayna hugs Murray while all three start to tear. Thomas fidgets and Shayna picks him up, showing him off to his new grandparents. Bella takes him in her arms smiling happily. Walter comes out and greets Shayna, too. They shake hands and Walter moves off to the side, unsure of himself, just as any seventeen-year-old would do as he stands alone between being a cool teenager and coming of age as an adult.

"I'll be eighteen real soon," Walter smiles.

Albert comes out of his room and stands in silence watching as Bella and Murray get reacquainted with their now twenty-four-year-old daughter and their new grandson. Shayna looks up, meeting Albert's eyes, as the bright sunlight shines through the open windows.

EPILOGUE

OPENED IN SEPTEMBER of 1941, the central tower at the Semlin Sajmiste Concentration Camp on the outskirts of Belgrade, Yugoslavia, looms like a monster in a child's nightmare. In due course, conditions eventually worsened in the camp to the point where it was matched in horror to Jasenovac and other large concentration camps. Semlin Sajmiste is where the male civilian prisoners from Banjica were sent, destined to use the transportation system of the central railway station nearby in Belgrade to distribute them to various points of labor and other camps throughout the occupied Balkans.

The camp was finally bombed in April 1944, by Allied and Partisan aircraft. Unfortunately, this resulted in killing many of the civilian inmates as well as the guards. At the end of the war, the camp's Commandant, Herbert Andorfer, managed to escape and flee to South America; he was at large until the sixties when he was finally apprehended in Austria. Andorfer and his Deputy Director, Edgar Enge were both arrested and given surprisingly light prison sentences for the murdering and torture of thousands of innocent people in the Semlin Sajmiste Camp. However, Deputy Commander Enge's prison sentence was never carried out due to his old age and poor health. In addition, many of the participating German and Serbian guards were never tried but served as witnesses in other trials most probably in deal exchanges for their freedom.

Semlin Sajmiste's name was later changed to Camp Zemun, although it originally had been an exhibition center and fairgrounds built by the Belgrade municipality in 1937. Its tall tower was initially built as a tourist attraction, and to transmit the earliest television broadcasts across Europe. With German occupation it morphed into a tombstone to the many thousands of hapless inmates, including children who unjustly lost their desperate lives under it.

Jasenovac Extermination Camp in Croatia was established in April of 1941, after the invasion of Yugoslavia. Called the Auschwitz of the Balkans, it was run by Croatian Fascists, racists, far-right ultra-nationalists and Croatian terrorist; it was built mainly to exterminate Serbian Communists, Partisans and religious / political opponents of the Nazi Regime and Fascist Roman Catholic Italy under Mussolini; local Jews, Gypsies and certain Muslims were not left out of the eradications.

Camp Jasenovac had no potable water for the prisoners to drink so they were forced to drink water from the Sava River, which was also used for bathing. Inmates had to relieve themselves in pits dug in the open fields covered in wooden planks from which they often fell or were pushed into. They were then left to drown in the sewerage which deliberately drained into the same river from which prisoners also drank.

The entire time of a Jasenovac inmate was much more terrifying than at either Banjica or Semlin Sajmiste because the Croatian guards were completely, sadistically insane. They enjoyed nightly contests where they would compete against each other for the most sadistic knife deaths of prisoners. Pure evil, they sometimes would even throw injured prisoners into the cremation pits with the dead just to watch them burn alive.

In April of 1945, the partisans entered Jasenovac too late as the guards had somehow been forewarned. The entire structure had subsequently been torched almost to the ground. After the war the site of the Jasenovac Camp was totally dismantled and leveled, erasing any traces of its physical existence forever. All that remains is lingering memories by the victim's extant friends and relatives and possibly the deceased restless spirits that may linger on remembering the ungodly terrors that took them to their horrific deaths at Jasenovac, pit of hell.

A monument now stands where the camp was, and visitors bring flowers when the sun shines dedicating them to the light and memory of those who suffered so greatly at Jasenovac. May God bless, remember and keep them.

After the war, Banjica's German Commandant, Willie Friedrich, is tried for war crimes by a Yugoslavian Military Court in Belgrade and sentenced to death. Banjica's Administrator Svetozar Vujkovic is tried by Yugoslavian Communists and executed. Emperor Hirohito of Japan who presided over the invasion of China and other countries, the bombing of Pearl Harbor and the eventual surrender to the Allies, was never tried for war crimes, as many members of his Japanese government were.

After WW II, the Banjica Concentration Camp reverts back to its former usage as a barracks for the Royal Yugoslav Army and still functions as such to the present day. A small Holocaust Museum opened there in 1969 and presently stands intact.

Approximately 77,000 German citizens were killed for war resistance. Many of these Germans had served in government, the military or civil positions.

Approximately 1.5 million Jews fought in WW II. Approximately 500,000 Jews served in the Soviet Army during WW II. 5,000 Palestinian Jews volunteered their services in the Jewish Brigade as part of the British Army during WW II.

The Yugoslav Partisan Rebels were the most effective resistance movement in all of occupied Europe. By the end of the war they had grown to 800,000 strong.

Partisan founder Josip Broz Tito became the first President for life of Yugoslavia in 1974. Major General of Yugoslav People's Army Moshe Piada became President of the Yugoslavian Parliament in 1954. Unfortunately, Resistance Commander Stjepan Filipovic was captured and hanged by Axis forces in 1942 at the young age of twenty-six years old. All three of these men are People's Heroes of Yugoslavia.

Approximately 70–85 million people perished in World War II – nearly 3% of the 1940 world population among these are 1 to 2 million Americans, 1 to 2 million French Indochinese, 1 to 2 million Philippines, 1 to 2 million Yugoslavians, 2 to 3 million Indians, 2 to 3 million Japanese, 4 million Dutch East Indies, 5 to 6 million Jewish citizens, 5 to 6 million Polish, 5.6 to 5.8 million Ethnic Poles, 7 to 8 million Balkan Slavs, Ethnic Greeks and Serbian Civilians, 8 to 9 million Germans, 10 to 20 million People's Republic of China, 26.6 million Soviet Republic, and many more of varied tragic losses.

There exists a floor plan to the Royal Yugoslav (Banjica) Army Base online and many newsreel archival videos are now in the hands of online non-profit organizations and the many Holocaust Museums available on demand. The majority of the dramatic characters are fictional but FIVE, now deceased, are public domain and historically accurate military figures: Josip Broz Tito, Moshe Piade, Stjepan Filipovic, Willie Friedrich, and Svetozar Vujkovic.

All references to any of the above history can be found online.

THE END

ABOUT CAROLYN KAY DOSWELL

CAROLYN KAY DOSWELL is the owner of EBD Publishing ASCAP and is a writing partner in *Panther Sight Productions*. A former teacher with the Los Angeles Unified School District, Carolyn has put her writing expertise to good use, having co-written, "A Flower Grows," "An American Rises," "Birds of Paradise," and "Jaguar's Child," with John Loretto.

She's also co-composer of pop songs "Accident'ly on Purpose," and "Only Twenty-Four" with Robin Randall. She currently resides in Palm Springs, California.

ABOUT JOHN LORETTO

JOHN LORETTO WAS BORN in Washington Heights, New York City and grew up in New Jersey where as a young adult he worked for a car dealership and as an assistant special education teacher. In high school, and college, he began his acting and writing career becoming affiliated with *Beautiful People Owen Action Theater Conservatory, Dead End Tommy Action Theater Conservatory, Summer and Smoke John Action Theater Conservatory, Tea and Sympathy Tommy Action Theater Conservatory*, and *Totally Cool Willy Action Theater Conservatory*.

He also trained with *Action Theatre Conservatory; Expressions Unlimited, Bobbie Shaw Chance Workshop; Joel & Kathleen Improvisational*; etc. Mr. Loretto has written four (4) screenplays: "A Flower Grows," "An American Rises," "Birds of Paradise," and "Jaguar's Child"; a reality television show concept; and one (1) novel. Some of John's movie credits include: *Gay* (Short) – *Fluffer Boy – 2018; Ill Bad Day* (Short) – *Businessman* – 2016; Room for Rent (TV Series) – *Daniel* – 2012; *Mexican Gangster* – Brooklyn Bob – 2008; *Chicano Blood* (Video) – *Mobster 1* – 2008; *Every Move You Make* (Video) – *Anson Shine* – 2002; etc. He currently resides in Palm Springs, California.

ABOUT DR. MICHAEL BERENBAUM

DR. MICHAEL BERENBAUM is an American scholar, professor, rabbi, writer, and filmmaker, who specializes in the study of the Holocaust. He served as Deputy Director of the President's Commission on the Holocaust (1979–1980), Project Director of the United States Holocaust Memorial Museum (USHMM) (1988–1993), and Director of the USHMM's Holocaust Research Institute (1993–1997).

Berenbaum also played a leading role in the creation of the United States Holocaust Memorial and Museum (HSHMM) and the content of its permanent exhibition. From 1997 to 1999, he served as President and CEO of the Survivors of the Shoah Visual History Foundation, and subsequently (and currently) as Director of the Sigi Ziering Institute: *Exploring the Ethical and Religious Implications of the Holocaust,* located at the American Jewish University (formerly known as the University of Judaism), in Los Angeles, CA. His wife, Melissa Patack Berenbaum, is the Vice President and General Manager of the Motion Picture Association of America (MPAA), California Group, and President of the California chapter of the MPAA.

Berenbaum is the father of four children: Rabbi Ilana Berenbaum Grinblat, Phillip Lev Berenbaum, Joshua Boaz Berenbaum, and Mira Leza Berenbaum.

Social Media Links

Social Media:

Facebook –
- DonnaInk Publications:
  https://www.facebook.com/DonnaInkPublications

LinkedIn –
- **Carolyn Kay Doswell** - https://www.linkedin.com/in/carolyn-kay-doswell-7534332b
- DonnaInk Publications:
  https://www.linkedin.com/company/donnainkpublications

Pinterest –
- DonnaInk Publications:
  https://www.pinterest.com/DonnaInkPublications

Tik Tok –
- DonnaInk Publications: @donnainkpublications

Tumblr –
- DonnaInk Publications:
  https://www.tumblr.com/donnainkpublications

YouTube –
- DonnaInk Publications: @DonnaInkPublications

X –
- DonnaInk Publications: https://x.com/DonnaInk

A Flower Grows Merchandise

Fans of *A Flower Grows* can now bring a piece of the story into their everyday lives through our exclusive line of themed merchandise. Donna**Ink Publications** offers custom mouse-pads, mugs, t-shirts, and other keepsakes inspired by the novel's imagery and emotional landscape.

To place an order, simply email donnaink@gmail.com, identify the item you'd like, along with any needed details such as size, color, or special preferences. Please include your email address and USPS mailing address so an invoice can be prepared. Your invoice will outline the item cost along with any applicable shipping and tax.

These unique pieces allow readers to celebrate the story while supporting the authors and the press that brought their work to life.

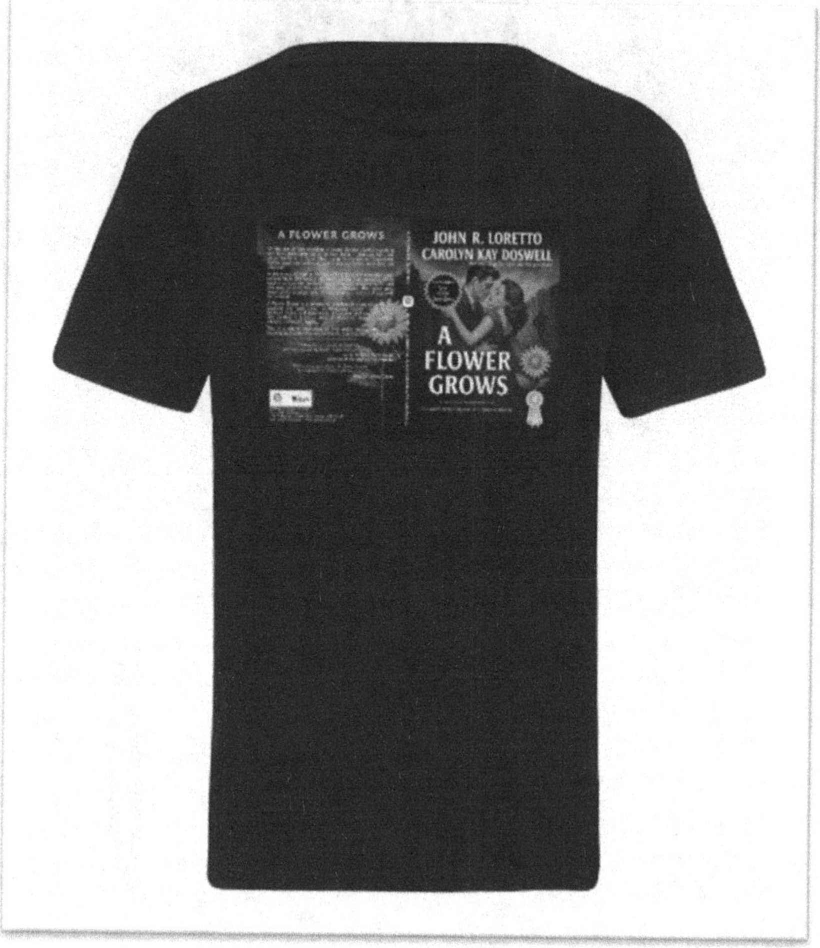
A FLOWER GROWS
JOHN R. LORETTO
CAROLYN KAY DOSWELL
A
FLOWER
GROWS

Moondust Media

Moondust Media

Donnaink Publications, L.L.C.